A SUMMER ON BELLEVUE AVENUE

ROMANCE AT THE GILDED AGE RESORTS
BOOK SIX

LORRI DUDLEY

WILD HEART
BOOKS

ISBN-13: 978-1-942265-88-7

"Perhaps you have come to royal dignity for just such a time as this?"

— ESTHER 4:14

CHAPTER 1

NEW YORK, NEW YORK
JUNE 7, 1895

a scream and tumbling sound woke Wesley Astor Jansen. He jolted upright from his desk and swiped at the paper that stuck to his cheek.

Had he dreamed the noise? Who else was here?

He tilted his ear up and listened, but in the office of Jansen and Sons Oil and Energy Engineering, not even the janitorial staff stirred. The oil lamp on the corner of his desk burned low. He flicked open his gold pocket watch and held it near the sputtering light.

Quarter after three in the morning. He snapped the lid shut and tucked the timepiece back into his suit pocket.

His copy of the signed marriage agreement he'd struggled for the better part of an hour to read through lay scattered across his desk. He gathered the pages into a pile and turned to file them in his side drawer.

Odd. The drawer stood open. Had he left it that way?

He slid the papers into the first folder, then closed and locked the compartment. It was late. He should head home. Light sparkled off the remaining bubbles still bursting in his half-finished champagne glass. He brought the glass over to the sideboard for the staff to clear.

It had been a solitary victory celebration after obtaining Mr. Klein's blessing to marry his daughter—a hard-won feat. Mr. Klein's ruthless business and social dealings sought one-sided advantages, but Wesley, too, could be relentless. A financial investment closed the deal with Klein & Co. manufacturing their line of motor cars with Jansen and Sons' unique grade of gasoline. They both signed, and the only stipulation was for Wesley's money to be returned if Amanda declined his offer of marriage.

Paying for his bride didn't sit well with Wesley. If Amanda discovered what her father asked of him and the dollar amount, she'd be horrified. In the end, he'd have paid even more because he loved Amanda, and a Jansen-Klein business alliance would profit them both.

Grander festivities would take place tomorrow evening after he proposed and Amanda accepted.

Wesley yawned and ran his hand down his face. He'd been having some dream. Amanda had slipped away for a reprieve from gathered guests and stood on the balcony of his New York City mansion peering down at Central Park below. Her dark hair was pulled up and woven with tiny pearls. Her long, graceful neck beckoned to be nuzzled. The silk material of her gown ruffled in the night breeze, emphasizing her delicate curves.

He touched the small of her back. She turned, greeting him with that shy smile of hers that slowly widened, until she glowed like the full moon. Few people witnessed Amanda's true joy—tiny, polite grins, yes—but he was one of the few blessed to feel the full radiance of her smile and laughter.

He swooped in and stole a kiss, brushing her velvet lips with his, and a thrill ran through his midsection like a player crossing the goal line. He couldn't wait to give her his last name and wake each morning with her beside him, tussled and sleepy-eyed. He leaned in to deepen their kiss, craving her feminine softness. The railing broke, and she screamed. His arms swiped air, and she tumbled into darkness below.

The scream must have been part of his dream, but by Jove, it had sounded real.

A groan resounded outside his office, raising the fine hair on his neck.

Wesley jumped to his feet and grabbed the oil lamp. He darted from the room and peered over the banister of the office's second-story gallery down into the open foyer below. "Who's there?"

Retreating footsteps slapped the tile floor of the

back hall, and a door slammed. Wesley turned to give chase, but a moan below stopped him.

Someone was hurt.

He leaned over the railing and extended the lamp out past his head. A form lay crumpled at the bottom of the curved stairs. Her skirts twisted around her body, and her leg bent at an odd angle.

Wesley dashed down the plush red carpet lining the marble stairs. He dropped to his knees next to the woman sprawled on her stomach on the cold tile.

"Are you all right?" Of course, she wasn't. He brushed her hair away from her face but didn't recognize her.

Her eyelashes fluttered, and a moan issued through her red lips.

Should he move her? Flip her over? "Where are you hurt?"

Her eyelids stopped moving.

He shook her, but she made no sound or movement. His hands quaked as he felt for her pulse, and he held his breath. A steady throb thumped against his fingertips.

Thank God.

His heart banged against his ribcage, vibrating his entire being. He jumped to his feet. Who would he find at this hour to aid her? The quiet foyer and empty building mocked him. The doctor lived five streets over, but was it wise to leave her? He ran to the entrance and flung open the main doors, the same ones he'd locked after letting himself in.

He leaned out into the damp night air. A street cleaner pushed his cart along Fifth Avenue, and a drunk couple clung to each other, stumbling into a back alley.

"You, there." He pointed to the street cleaner. "Twenty dollars awaits you if you fetch Doctor Collins on Fifty-Ninth and Sixth."

The street cleaner dropped his broom and ran.

"Twenty dollars, you say?" The other man pushed away from the woman and sprinted remarkably well in his drunken state toward Fifty-Ninth.

"Cad." The woman spat in the man's wake and stomped down the side street.

Wesley re-entered the lobby. He grabbed another lamp, and turning the wick up, knelt beside the woman.

She dressed formally as if she'd attended a performance at the Metropolitan Opera House, but seated in the pit, not the upscale balcony box seats. A plume of feathers protruded from a cockeyed hat, askew from her fall. Rouge stained her cheeks and lips.

Who was she? A customer who'd been locked inside? A robber or thief? Someone had run. Had that been her accomplice?

He shrugged off his jacket and folded it into a square. Gently lifting her head, he slid the makeshift pillow underneath so her face no longer lay on the cold marble tile. He scooted back to put a hand's length between them.

What kind of gossip would spread about such a woman found sprawled on the floor of Jansen and Sons? Would it affect business? His reputation?

Wesley's stomach soured.

Would it affect Mr. Klein's blessing to marry Amanda?

Surely, once the woman woke, she'd explain to the authorities why she was here and what she'd been doing. He'd been asleep, but that weak alibi wouldn't be enough to squash any rumors.

The image of his open desk drawer flashed in his memory, and a troubling premonition slithered down his spine. If she'd fallen down the stairs, then she must have been on the same floor as him. Had she been in his office?

Wesley glanced over his shoulder. A slipper lay about halfway up the stairs. He retrieved it, laying it next to the woman. A reticule was hooked on her arm, and a paper stuck out of the top bearing the Jansen company letterhead symbol. He loosened the drawstring and peeked within.

Several papers had been folded and shoved inside. He removed them and flipped through the pages. A company balance sheet and income statement lay among some of the proprietary paperwork. He recognized double-underlined numbers, and the corresponding lines showed the company's total equity and net income. Behind those reports, he found what resembled stock purchases, though the words were difficult to make out, and the negotiated gentleman's agreement between Klein & Co. and Jansen and Sons that he'd signed tonight.

Was she a competitor's spy or sent by a labor union leader to rally support for a strike? These weren't merely from his files but also his brother's—the head of marketing and sales. He stared at the unconscious woman in a new light. She'd been trying to bamboozle them.

Where was the doctor?

He stomped to the front door and flung it wide. The doctor's coach barreled down the street, and the horses skidded to a stop in front of the building. The carriage door was flung open, and the doctor exited with black bag in hand, still buttoning his coat.

"Doctor Collins." Wesley waved. "Right this way." He gestured to the lobby and stepped aside to let the man pass.

The doctor pushed up his spectacles and knelt beside the woman. "What happened here?" He lifted her wrist, felt for a pulse, and nodded.

Wesley shrugged. "I fell asleep at my desk, awoke to a scream, and found her like this."

"I see." He moved the lamp closer to her face and pulled her eyelids apart. He peered into each eye. "Was she conscious?"

"Not entirely. She moaned a few times." Wesley

stepped back and leaned on the curved newel post at the bottom of the stairs.

"We'll need to get her to the hospital." He nodded to the door. "Tell my coachman to bring the stretcher."

Wesley jumped at the chance to feel useful and to leave the bizarre scene before him. The coachman and footman retrieved the stretcher, and Wesley held the door open for them to pass.

"Her tibia appears broken. We must flip her over, but I'll need to stabilize the leg. Mr. Jansen, please hold her head, and my coachman and footman will handle the heavy lifting."

Wesley crouched, and on the count of three, adjusted the woman's head as they guided her onto the stretcher.

The doctor sent a footman back to the carriage for a brace while he checked the woman over for any other sustained injuries.

An officer appeared in the open entrance and rapped on the door. "I saw the doctor's coach and the lamplight through the window. Is there a problem?" He crossed his arms and glared at Wesley as if he'd already been condemned without a trial.

A cold prickle raised the hairs on the back of his neck.

"Who's the lady?" The officer inclined his head toward the stretcher.

"I don't have the foggiest." Wesley recounted his story, including the papers found in her reticule, but as he envisioned the events through the eyes of the officer, the alarm sounding in Wesley's mind increased.

A nicely dressed woman lay on the floor, unconscious, her hair mussed and lipstick smudged, which likely had happened during the fall but had the look of being smeared during a midnight tryst. The officer asked where Wesley had been, and he showed his workspace where he'd fallen asleep on his desk. The officer's gaze lingered on the half-drunk champagne glass. He closed the office door as they exited. To prevent evidence tampering?

"You're considering this a crime scene?" Wesley hated the squeak in his voice.

What would happen when word spread? How would it affect Jansen and Sons' reputation and business dealings—especially the promotion of their new gasoline? What about Amanda? Her father? Their engagement to be announced? He placed his hand on the wall to not double over at the sick feeling in his stomach.

The officer's lips twisted into a sardonic smile. "Don't worry. Someone's father will pay to have this slid under the rug. Someone always does with you knickerbocker types."

"What about the documents in her purse?"

"Easily could have been planted." The officer held Wesley's gaze.

Wesley refused to squirm. "But they weren't."

Below, the men lifted the stretcher and carried the

woman out of the lobby. The officer trotted down the stairs and exited the building. Wesley followed. Morning sun crested the horizon, but overcast clouds turned the sky an eerie yellow-gray and hazed the glow of the oil lamps lining the street.

A spitting drizzle of late spring clung to Wesley's white linen tuxedo shirt, and cold seeped through without his jacket to warm him.

The woman on the stretcher stirred.

Wesley stepped closer, curious for a better look at the woman's alert face.

Her eyes opened, and she blinked as if trying to focus. "Why?" She snatched his shirtfront and twisted her grip.

"Who are you?" Wesley pulled back, but the woman held him with surprising strength.

"You said you loved me."

She mistook him for someone else. Maybe the man who ran out the back. "How did you get in the building?" He pried her fingers away. "Who accompanied you?"

Her eyes rolled back in her head, and her hand dropped.

He held the side of the stretcher, stalling footmen carrying her. "What were you doing here?"

The officer pulled him away, and she was loaded into the bed of the carriage. The doctor climbed inside and closed the door.

The street sweeper lingered about, waiting for

payment, and Wesley pulled out a twenty-dollar bill and passed it to him.

A stranger who'd stood beside the doctor flipped a page of his notepad. "Mr. Jansen." He stepped forward. "Who was that woman, and how did she get injured?"

"I've never seen her before in my life." Bile rose in Wesley's throat.

"Why were you working so late at night?"

Wesley strode back into the building, unable to block the niggling that there was something familiar about the woman's face, nor the foreboding that his life had been ruined. He was used to talking his way out of debacles. As chief executive of operations, he'd finagled his way through negotiations, contracts, and lawsuits. He knew how to think fast and when to bluff or show his hand, but this fiasco landed a left hook from out of nowhere.

He peered up at the chandelier dripping with crystals and dangling from the gold-leafed circle pendant and beseeched God. "Why now? Why, with so much hanging in the balance?"

Amanda.

The way the reporter's lips had curved, like a fox licking its lips, built pressure in Wesley's chest. He must explain the truth to Amanda before vicious gossip or the morning paper reached her. He grabbed his jacket off the floor, bolted up the stairs to his office, retrieving his hat, and rushed back down.

"Whoa, now. Where are you off to so fast?" The officer stood in the open foyer.

Wesley slowed his descent. "Sir?"

The loathing in the officer's gaze turned Wesley's stomach.

"The name's Detective Millis." He folded his arms. "And I have more questions for you."

CHAPTER 2

"*A*manda Mae Klein!" Her aunt's impatient screech rose above the rain's patter on the glass ceiling.

Amanda ignored her aunt's call echoing through the main house and under the solarium's door and pruned one last branch off the fragrant white gardenia bush. Her precious quiet time alone in the glass fortress of the hot house, away from social settings, expectations, and prying eyes was her respite. She forbade all staff from entering her sacred space, preferring to clean her own messes than to share this time with anyone other than God.

Her gloved fingers scooped a handful of rich, composted soil and added it to the newly potted plant. The earthy aroma blended with the gardenia's green-peach scent, reminding her of lying in the grass and warm sunshine while her beloved governess read Bible stories of love and courage.

Amanda removed her gardening gloves, then she untied her apron and hung it on a peg. She inhaled one last breath of the verdant, humid air and opened the door to the main house.

"There you are." Aunt Sally halted in mounting the back stairs and fanned her flushed face so rapidly that her diamond pendant earrings swung back and forth. "Mrs. Van Hassel is in the blue salon. Entertain her while I oversee the packing. We must leave for Newport at once."

"Leave?" In this downpour?

Aunt Sally gripped the banister. Her ample bosom strained against the bodice of her gown with each breath. "There is no time to swoon, so don't even think about it."

Swoon? Amanda's brows pulled together. What had come over her aunt?

"Clara?" Aunt Sally called the parlor maid. "Where are you? Off dilly-dallying again, I take it."

Amanda didn't defend the hardworking servant but flashed Clara what she hoped was a sympathetic warning that Aunt Sally was in one of her tizzies.

"Yes, miss?" Clara scurried into the back hall, holding a feather duster in her hand.

"Assist me upstairs." Aunt Sally leaned on the maid's arm as if incapable of climbing the stairs on her own, which she'd managed fine less than twenty minutes ago.

Clara guided Aunt Sally upstairs.

Amanda checked for dirt smudges on her gown. Olivia Van Hassel was a stickler for propriety. Like the Kleins, Olivia's family came from old money, and Olivia had married into the same. She'd reprimanded Amanda on several occasions that society walkers must hold themselves to a higher standard, to which those in obscurity could strive toward.

A footman rounded the corner carrying a large paper package with an extravagant bow. "This arrived for you, miss." He set it on the half-round table under the gilded mirror and handed her the corresponding card.

Wesley. Amanda's lips curved into a smile. It must be from him. He'd been acting secretive and most pleased with himself at the Breslin party. At her parting, he'd leaned in so close his lips brushed her cheek and whispered, "I have much in store for you tomorrow. Rest well, my heart."

Her stomach swirled as it had last evening when he'd boldly breathed the endearment. She flipped the card over and read the broad-scripted capital *W*. Wesley had never been one for correspondence, instead choosing to verbalize his sentiments.

She melted whenever he called her his *Mandi Mae,* and she replayed last night's words, engraving them into her memory. *I'm restless—a complete bore—without you lighting up my day. I ache to hear your laughter and see your face. Mandi Mae, you own my heart.*

The first time he conveyed similar thoughts, she'd laughed, believing him nonsensical, but his persistent pursuit proved his feelings to be genuine. Her lips curved into a smile, and she tugged on the package's taffeta ribbon and nodded for the footman to aid her in carefully peeling back the paper.

She gasped at the double arch of bright magenta flowers. "An orchid." The rare flowering plant was her favorite but had to be imported from the Leeward Islands and carefully maintained in transport. What lengths he must have gone to acquire the precious plant. She fingered the fragile flower.

"Shall I water it in the kitchen?" The footman gripped the pot in both hands.

"Leave it here. Orchids need special care. I'll take it to the hot house after I meet with Mrs. Van Hassel."

Amanda checked the hall clock. Half past nine in the morning.

A jolt straightened her spine. For Olivia to be awake at what she considered "an unholy hour intended for ordinary mortals" meant something was amiss.

The footman pushed open the door to the blue salon for Amanda to enter.

Olivia perched on the tufted sofa, dressed in a morning gown of cream satin with ruffled lace that cascaded to the floor.

"I came as soon as I heard." Oliva's aloof expression offered no context for her words.

Amanda rang the bell pull. "Heard what, exactly?"

"Don't bother. There's isn't time for tea." Olivia rose and crossed the room, taking Amanda's hands as she'd often done in boarding school. "If we act quickly, disaster can be averted."

An echo from Amanda's past blared in her mind. "The carriage your father sent has arrived for you, and we must act quickly." Lily, her governess, had knelt before her with tears in her eyes. "He's enrolled you in a prestigious boarding school for ladies. It's a splendid opportunity."

"I don't want to go. I want to stay here with you. Please don't make me."

Lily had wrapped Amanda in a tight embrace and whispered in her ear. "Darling, there is good to be found everywhere. God has prepared you for this moment. Go and bloom where you are planted, because He has tilled the soil."

A piece of Amanda's heart had severed as her father's carriage had pulled away from Lily's quaint home in Virginia with Amanda ensconced inside. She'd watched the woman who'd taken her mother's place long before Amanda's mother had been pronounced dead fade into the distance.

Amanda swallowed old apprehensions of a young girl on the cusp of womanhood and braced for whatever emergency had arisen. She met Olivia's gaze. "What disaster?"

"Thank heaven, my maid heard the news and thought to wake me."

"What news?" The toast and jam Amanda had for breakfast turned to lead in her stomach.

"The man she's sweet upon works at the *Herald*, so you're fortunate to be able to have a leg up on the ordeal before gossip spreads."

Amanda's volume rose. "What ordeal?"

Olivia warned her with a glare that clearly said it wasn't proper to raise one's voice. "A woman tumbled down the stairs at Jansen and Sons last night." She patted Amanda's hand. "Wesley was with her—alone."

Amanda sank onto the arm of the wingback chair as Olivia conveyed the details of the article. Awful images of Wesley in another woman's arms superimposed over the memory of Wesley's grin and firm hold as he swept Amanda across the dance floor last evening. The warmth in his eyes as he guided her up the stairs, allowing her a respite from socializing, merged with a woman tumbling to the landing below. Their stolen moments when he called her his Mandi Mae, whispered endearments, and pressed a gentle kiss to her cheek became tainted by the image of a woman gripping his shirt front, pleading to understand because she thought he loved her.

Amanda wrapped her arms about her stomach. *Mandi Mae* whispered in her conscience. "Wesley wouldn't..." She shook her head, and the patterned rug blurred before her eyes. "It can't be." Wesley's smile—the one that made her feel as though it was just she and him in all of New York—flickered in her memory. "Wesley wouldn't do that to me."

"It doesn't matter if he would or wouldn't. You must worry about perceptions." Olivia paced the length of the Oriental rug. "The one saving grace is that even though Mr. Jansen had already spoken to your father, he hasn't actually proposed to you yet."

Amanda's gaze riveted on Olivia. "He what?"

"I heard it from my husband, who pressed his ear to the door when Mr. Jansen asked for a moment with your father. Jeffrey believed they might be discussing stock tips but landed that juicy bit of gossip instead."

Wesley had been about to propose?

Amanda's stomach swallowed her heart. Her Wesley? The man in whom she'd confided her deepest fears? The same man who swooped in at social events to rescue her when words wouldn't come or when all gazes pivoted in her direction and her heartbeat thundered in her ears? He'd been about to propose to her, but then ran around with some fast woman and started a horrid scandal?

"Don't get woozy." Olivia snapped her fingers. "As I told your aunt, there is no time for fainting. You must leave for Newport immediately and beat the delivery of the morning paper. Everyone will come calling, wanting to be the first to witness your reaction." She aided Amanda to a stand and ushered her toward the door.

Amanda pulled back. "I must speak to Wesley and hear the truth."

"Are you listening? The man is a blooming bounder."

"I need to hear it from him."

"There isn't time." Olivia slapped her hands against the sides of her skirts.

"If I leave, he'll appear guilty."

"The circumstances make him look guilty. He was caught alone with Miss Cynthia Blunt, a loose moral social climber, in the middle of the night. Whether they argued and he pushed her down the stairs is what remains to be determined."

The name sounded familiar, but Amanda's recollection hazed. Did it matter who? She pressed her hand to her throat. The same man who proclaimed his loyal devotion, who treated her with respect and spoke of their future together with rapt delight, couldn't be capable of such a dastardly act. She shook her head. "Wesley wouldn't."

Olivia stamped her foot. "I know how you are with crowds. Do you really want to be here when all of New York's gossipmongers come knocking, fill your parlor, and press you for the sordid details?"

The tips of Amanda's ears burned as the aftermath of her mother's affair resurfaced. Neighbors, friends, and acquaintances had whispered behind their gloves and stared at Amanda whenever she'd left the house. Snide snickers followed her wherever she went, and a few bold gossip hounds blocked her way, demanding information as a toll to pass.

Amanda's knees threatened to topple. She tried to sit but Olivia held her steady.

"Go to Newport." Olivia's gloved hands cupped Amanda's cheeks. "I have an event today but will follow you tomorrow. The summer's heat arrived early, and all of New York's elite will be relocating to their cottages soon, anyway. Your trip will look planned, and you can receive word of the situation without being thrown into the thick of it."

Amanda nodded, even though her heart cried for truth.

"Besides, you can't handle another scandal after what your mother put you through."

"No." Amanda's voice reduced to a mere whisper. "I couldn't bear it."

Olivia guided her to the door. "Your aunt is seeing to your packing. You should go to the carriage and wait for her. I'll speed things along."

She ushered Amanda into the hall and placed her hands on Amanda's shoulders. "Everything will die down after a few weeks. These things always do." She released Amanda and climbed the back stairs after Aunt Sally.

A cold hollowness scraped away at Amanda's insides until only a fragile shell remained.

Wesley.

She gripped the edge of a table, afraid she might shatter. The thick leaf of the orchid brushed her hand, and a sob escaped her lips. Wesley wouldn't do this to her, would he? What of his words? What of his professions of love? Did they mean nothing?

A maid passed, carrying an armload of gowns.

Amanda straightened and blinked away her tears. She mustn't draw attention. As she'd learned from her mother's scandal, people not only fed off gossip but also others' pain. Turning to a task-oriented mindset, she picked up the orchid and marched back into the hothouse. She instructed the gardener how to care for her plants while she was away.

Aunt Sally poked her head into the solarium. "There you are. Our trunks are packed, and the coachmen are ready to depart."

The gardener nodded to her arms. "What about that one? I've never seen the like."

Amanda glanced down at the orchid she'd forgotten she still held. She started to pass it to the gardener but recoiled, unwilling to let it go. "This one will remain with me."

"Come along, Amanda." Aunt Sally raised her voice. "It's time to leave."

In a numb daze, she followed her aunt out the front door, where the carriage awaited under the overhang with a second conveyance waiting behind it for their luggage and a select few of Aunt's personal staff. Even though their walk was covered, two footmen held umbrellas to block the blowing rain. Water ran off the coachman's hat brim, and he slunk deeper into his overcoat. One of the footmen aided her and Aunt Sally inside and closed the door behind them. Rain battered against the carriage roof.

Aunt Sally adjusted her bustle. "Thank heaven for Olivia Van Hassel. The credit shall be laid at her door if we avoid getting caught in this scandal. She is a true friend. You are fortunate to have made her acquaintance at finishing school and that she benevolently admitted you into the elite ranks as her protégé."

Amanda gripped the orchid pot tighter. The verbal barb ground against her frayed emotions. "I wasn't some country bumpkin. Lily had instilled in me all the necessary propriety and etiquette."

"It's one thing to learn about social skills from a governess and another to mingle among society without embarrassing the old-money nobs or appearing uncouth like the new-money swells. You should be grateful that Olivia polished any dinginess you might have picked up from the governess's household and allowed you into society's inner sanctum."

Whether she desired to be there or not.

Amanda swallowed her churlishness. If it hadn't been for Olivia, she wouldn't have met Wesley—but then, she wouldn't be fleeing another scandal.

The carriage rocked forward, and Amanda gripped the side door for balance. Raindrops streaked the glass, blurring Fifth Avenue into gray blobs. A darker gray shape drew closer. The coachman pulled onto the street, and the blob disappeared from view. A man hollered, but Amanda couldn't discern the words shouted over the pounding rain.

A palm pressed on the outside of the glass.

Amanda jerked back, and her aunt screamed.

"Amanda!"

She gasped. *Wesley?*

"Amanda, wait." He ran alongside the carriage, his body too close to the wheels.

"Stop the carriage." Amanda shifted in her seat. Wesley's handsome face with wet locks of hair clinging to his forehead hovered within a few inches just outside.

"Keep going," Aunt Sally shouted. "Shoo." She waved a glove as if she could swat him away like a fly.

"Let me explain!" he yelled through the window.

"Be careful!" Amanda placed her hand on the glass matching his.

The coachman drove onward, and Wesley's hand slid down the pane.

Aunt Sally yanked Amanda's arm back. "You'll not draw my niece into your shenanigans."

"Amanda, please." He clung to the side of the coach. "I love you."

"Then why?" Her voice cracked from the lump in her throat. She loved him, too, and wanted to hear him out, but he knew her fear of scandal. How could he tear her in two like this?

His form slipped from view.

Amanda gasped and flipped around to kneel on the seat cushion, her bustle bumping Aunt Sally. She yanked aside the back curtain and peered out the window.

Wesley stood in the middle of the street, his hands pressed to the sides of his head. "Amanda!"

She hugged the orchid pot to her breast.

"Sit down, young lady. That is not how a proper woman conducts herself." Aunt Sally tugged on Amanda's arm, but she ignored her. "How dare Mr. Jansen bring his scandal to our doorstep?" She folded her arms. "The entire neighborhood heard him cry your name."

Amanda stared at Wesley's anguished form, frozen in the middle of the street with coachmen guiding their carriages around him. The Klein driver steered the horses and carriage down Thirty-eighth Street, and Amanda resettled forward, leaning her head against the side of the window. Tears streamed over her cheeks as raindrops trickled down the glass. Would a scandal hurt more than losing her heart?

CHAPTER 3

"Get out of the road, you corned bugger!"

Wesley stumbled out of the way of a hackneyed cab barreling along Fifth Avenue. The agony on Amanda's face and the Klein set of coaches pulling out of sight could mean only one thing. Gossip had already reached her ears.

Blast. Amanda would run from a scandal, and who would blame her after the public ruckus her mother's infidelity caused? He retrieved his felt Homburg hat from a puddle. A wagon wheel imprint left it badly misshapen, but he punched the hat back into proper form and plopped it on his head. If only he could beat his life back into some semblance of what it was yesterday. How could he fall asleep celebrating Mr. Klein's marital blessing, and the next morning, wake to Amanda fleeing the city—and him? He splashed through a puddle, not caring that his leather shoes and wool suit were ruined, and staggered onto the sidewalk.

A man with his trench coat collar points raised and his bowler hat pulled low bumped Wesley as he rushed by.

The pain in Wesley's shoulder didn't compare to the deep ache in his heart. There had to be a way to fix this. By Jove, he hadn't done anything wrong, but it didn't matter. Detective Millis and Doctor Collins had peered at him with suspicion, and Amanda had left with two coaches, which meant they didn't plan to return until summer's end. His chest constricted and he struggled to breathe. Despite the rain, he loosened the top buttons of his shirt and leaned against the stone stair post of the Klein's New York home.

If Detective Millis hadn't detained him for so long, he could have spoken to Amanda. Now he had to find a way to convince Amanda, her father, and the public of the truth while they summered in Newport.

A rivet of rain found a way underneath his collar and ran cold down his back. He pushed off the stone railing and stumbled along the sidewalk. He needed to think, form a plan. Challenges weren't new to him. *Lord, You've pulled me out of more situations than I can count. Guide me through this one.*

It wasn't until he turned up the steps to his older brother's townhouse that Wesley even realized he'd headed there. Theo would know what to do. His big brother could handle this.

He peered up at the rain plummeting to the earth and whispered, "Thank You, Lord, for directing my steps here."

He rapped the brass knocker on the thick oak panel.

Theo's stern-looking butler opened the door a hand's width. "Mr. Jansen." His gaze roved over Wesley's drenched form.

"Is Theodore in?"

The butler swung the entrance wider and gestured for Wesley to come in. "I'm afraid he's still resting, sir."

Wesley slumped against the door's frame and fished in his pocket for his calling card. He passed the now damp and wavy rectangle with his initials to the butler. "Tell him I called." He'd go home and try to make heads or tails of the strange chicanery in which he found himself."

"Uncle Wes." His young nephew, Samuel, already resembling the Jansen male line with his thick waves of hair, oblong face, and tall frame, hopped off the tricycle he'd been riding across the checkered marble floor and ran to the door. Squeezing around the butler's legs, he said, "I lost a tooth." He pushed his lower jaw forward and pointed to the gap in the front. "See."

Despite his foul mood, Wesley forced a smile for his beloved nephew. "How's that going to affect your whistle?"

Sam frowned, puckered his lips, and blew. An airy wheeze sputtered but turned into a sharp, shrill toot. "It's still there."

Little footsteps sounded behind Sam. The boy's younger sister, Ana, toddled over with her hands held out for balance, her fine hair pulled into a single bow on the crown of her head and her linen dress already sporting a drool stain on the front.

Ana spied her uncle, broke into a big smile, and precariously tottered over and gripped his pant leg.

He lifted her into the air. "Don't grow up." He planted a kiss on her cheek. "Stay happy and innocent for as long as you can. For the world will try to steal it from you." Wesley set her back down lest his drenched clothes soak her. He turned to leave.

"Wesley, is that you?" Clarissa rounded the corner, her blond hair sleeked back into a twist. She wore a light spring gown, but the fashionable narrow waist had been tailored to accommodate her rounding belly for their third child. "What happened? You look like a drenched mudsill, returning from a rough day of street sweeping." She waived him farther inside, and her gaze narrowed on his head. "Are those wagon wheel marks on your hat?"

He stepped back into the foyer, careful to stay on the rug and not leave a puddle on their polished floors.

The butler removed Wesley's wet overcoat and hat.

Clarissa passed the children to their nanny, who stood in the far corner next to a Greek statue of Hera. Had the silent nursemaid been there the whole time? Clarissa waved him into the next room. "Come and dry yourself by the fire."

She hooked her arm around Wesley's, not accepting no for an answer, and led him into the adjoining salon next to the hearth. A maid entered and draped a towel over Wesley's shoulders before adding a log to the flames.

"Do tell." Clarissa positioned herself on the opposite end of the mantel and rested her laced fingers upon her rounded stomach.

"I was hoping to get Theo's advice on a situation." He scraped his damp hair off his forehead. "I'm in a bind and truly don't know how it all happened."

Her lips pursed. "Theo's been out all night, first the Breslin party and then joined his friends at the club. He stumbled in at an early-morning hour." She huffed a deep sigh. "I imagine he'll wake with a pounding headache, forcing me to keep the blinds drawn and the children quiet all day."

When Wesley had invited Theo to join him in celebrating his pre-engagement to Amanda, Theo had declined, saying Clarissa was expecting him home early. Wesley refused to be offended that his brother went to the men's Knickerbocker Club to drink instead. Theo enjoyed his liquor, and Wesley didn't care much for the stuff.

"I doubt he'll be up before noon, but"—her gaze softened—"I'm happy to listen."

Clarissa was a good soul, and Theo was lucky to have her. There weren't too many love matches among the younger set. The trend was for parents to marry off their rich heiress daughters to financially bail out the British aristocracy in exchange for a noble title. It had taken Wesley his best sales pitch to convince Mr. Klein to allow Amanda to marry him and not wed her to a British noble fop.

Wesley's shoulders slumped. This morning's incident and the scandalous gossip that was sure to follow would negate all his work to gain not just Mr. Klein's favor but Amanda's too.

Clarissa cast a glance at a footman, and the man rushed to bring a bishop's chair for Wesley to sit upon near the fire. With a second look from Clarissa, the footman backed out of the room with the remainder of the servants and closed the door.

"It's difficult for me to stand for too long in my condition." Clarissa lowered onto the couch. "I can tell something is weighing heavily on you. I promise it won't leave this room."

Wesley sat and rubbed his face. Perhaps a woman's perspective would help. "I fell asleep last night working in my office and awoke to a woman's scream." He relayed the morning's events, but Clarissa's horrified expression didn't settle his nerves.

"I can't lose Amanda. I love her." He stared into the flames. "She's beautiful, smart, and kind. If she disappears at a party, I can almost guarantee she's either in the gardens, discussing plants with the gardener, or in the library, researching a question from an overheard discussion. I'm awed by her calm grace and sensitivity."

He snorted. "She even appreciates my boldness and ease with conversation. She listens and is perceptive, too, noticing people's moods and anonymously sending flowers to cheer them. She even sent herbs for Mrs. Astor's maid who kept sneezing."

He closed his eyes, fighting the tightness in his chest. "I envisioned her by my side, entertaining business contacts, having children, growing old together, building a legacy." He moaned a deep guttural sound like a wounded animal. "Last night, I asked her father for her hand in marriage."

Clarissa gasped.

Wesley opened his eyes with a sigh. "The first thing I did once the police released me was to run to her house to explain what happened, but someone beat me to it. The Kleins packed two coaches and left, likely to stay in Newport for the entire summer." His voice cracked. "I can't comprehend how this could happen. Who was the woman who fell? Why was she in the office after hours? I need to understand."

"I can help with that." Clarissa lifted her chin. "I have a special talent for getting tongues wagging."

"It seems I've been framed. I played no part in this, but retelling the story, even *I* think I sound guilty." Wesley rubbed the tension out of the back of his neck. "What do I do? I can't lose her."

A firmness lit Clarissa's eyes, and she pursed her lips. "You truly love her?"

"I do." His hoarse whisper rang with authenticity.

Clarissa stood and walked over to a desk and removed a key. "Then go to her." She gripped his hand and turned it, pressing the metal into his open palm. "It's the key to Tiverton Bluff in Newport—my family's holdings."

He stared at the shiny brass.

"Go to her. She's right to be awed by your charm. No one is gifted with words as much as you." She smiled. "You could persuade a snake into buying shoes. Convince her of your side of the story. Show her how much you love her."

Clarissa was right. He'd never cowered from a challenge before. Why would he now when his heart lay in the balance? His chest lifted but then fell. "What about the woman who's in the hospital? I've told all I know to the police, but shouldn't I at least stay until I know she's all right?"

"Theo will check on her for you, and if her health declines, we'll send for you immediately."

He stood, gripped the sides of Clarissa's face, and pressed a kiss on the crown of her head. "You're a godsend." He stepped back and grinned, feeling as if fresh air filled his lungs. "Theo is one lucky fellow to have you. Married above his grade, if you ask me. I'm fortunate to have found someone similar, and I won't let Amanda go without a fight."

He strode to the door and paused before exiting. "Thank you." He held up the key. "First, I'm going to convince Amanda to marry me. Then I'll convince her to name our first-born daughter after you."

"I'm going to hold you to that." Clarissa's teasing voice followed him into the foyer.

The butler handed Wesley his coat and hat.

"Wesley?" A groggy Theo leaned over the second-story railing.

"I can't talk now. Clarissa can fill you in. Off to Newport"—he tipped his hat—"but thanks for checking on the woman."

Theo's bottom lip trembled as if he struggled for words. "What wo-woman?"

"The one in the hospital." Wesley waved farewell and slipped out the door. The sooner Amanda could hear him out, the sooner his life could get back on track.

CHAPTER 4

NEWPORT, RHODE ISLAND
JUNE 8, 1895

*a*manda awoke to a maid drawing the curtains
and broad daylight spilling across an Axmin-
ster rug. She murmured, "What time is it?" before
rolling over and pressing her face into the down pillow.

"Noon, miss," said a young voice that wasn't the
typical housemaid who drew open her curtains in New
York.

Amanda turned her head and squinted one eye
open. It took a few moments for her brain to recognize
her surroundings as her bedchamber in Breakwater
Court, their Newport summer home. Her room resembled an English garden with floral curtains and wainscoted walls painted a pale green with darker trim.

A newly hired lady's maid stood in the corner awaiting direction. Her springy red curls spilled out from under her white cap.

Newport.

A rush of memories from eons ago, back when her mother used to bring her here for the summer, flooded her heart. The manor she'd visited had been only a cottage before a fire burnt it to the ground and her father had it rebuilt to rival a French chateau. She'd spent the days swimming in the ocean and playing in the sand with the local children while her mother ventured out on yachts and socialized with captains and exotic travelers.

Amanda inhaled the sea air drifting through the window laced with promise until the remembrance of why she'd arrived choked the air from her lungs.

She rolled to her back and pressed the pillow over her face to block out the image of Wesley holding another woman—kissing another woman. Was this how her father felt when he learned Mother had run off with Captain Adams?

She screamed into the feathers.

"Miss?"

Amanda stilled. The maid's presence had slipped her mind.

She peeked from under the pillow to see the crisp skirt of the servant and a tray with Amanda's morning coffee. Aunt Sally must be awake and instructing the staff.

"The name's Katie. If ya need anything, miss." She held the breakfast tray toward Amanda.

Amanda scooted upright in bed and tucked the pillow behind her back. She accepted the tray, and her lips parted to...apologize? Thank her for the tray? Expressing one's gratitude would have been expected in Lily's household, but Olivia and Aunt Sally would click their tongues in disapproval at thanking a servant for doing their job.

"I'm not much fer mornin's either." Katie moved to the wardrobe and removed a lavender day gown with tiered ruffles down the skirt. "Not until I've had a cup of coffee."

Amanda enjoyed the quiet of dawn and rarely slept late, but they'd disembarked around two in the morning after an entire day of travel by rail, steam ship, and coach, and reached Breakwater Court by three. Having short notice of their arrival, the servants flew into a frenzy to prepare the premises for her aunt and herself, and another hour had passed before their rooms were ready. Amanda had tried to rest or read in the private rail car, but her mind had tortured her with thoughts of Wesley, and even aboard the steamship that brought them into Newport Harbor, all she could see in the swirling water was her future being sucked into darkness's deep depths.

Katie laid out a brush, comb, and ribbon that matched the lavender dress. Amanda floundered for small talk, so she remained quiet. Katie went about her duties, fixing Amanda's hair while Amanda finished her coffee.

"I'm afraid you missed the luncheon for the early Newport arrivers on Mr. Noble's yacht this morning." Katie slid a pin into Amanda's coiffure. "I overheard this afternoon, your set will be watchin' the polo match. Will you be attendin', miss?"

Amanda exhaled. In her current state, she'd be poor company. She had no mind for the social drudgery of a polo match with a bunch of dear old ducks and clever fellows who wanted to speak of orders for their latest gowns cabled to arrive from Paris or their recent lucky turn in the stock market. A restlessness curled her toes. She wanted to hitch up her skirts and run until her heart pounded and she couldn't catch her breath, proving her heart remained in her chest and not an empty hole. Running was considered ill-mannered, but a gallop on horseback might quiet her agitated spirit.

She checked the clock on the mantel. Unfortunately, she'd missed the morning ride. Perhaps if she walked along the cliffs of Ochre Point? Her spirits already teetered on a precipice. Best not to skirt one in her current state.

"Archery," she blurted out the word and sat a little taller as the clever idea resonated. "I believe I shall practice my archery."

"Fine choice for such a lovely day." Katie retrieved a smart frock coat from the wardrobe along with a high-crown hat and archery gloves.

Amanda donned the items and strode down the carpeted hallway.

Aunt Sally's voice permeated her solid oak bedchamber door, berating a maid for missing the dust that had settled on the gilded frame of her portrait.

Picking up her pace, Amanda slipped down the curved staircase into the foyer.

A maid scurried past, carrying a bundle of fresh-cut irises and white lilies half the maid's size. She set the bouquet in a large cut-crystal vase on the rosewood table in the center of the room.

The clicking of Amanda's heels on the marble tile floors alerted the maid to her presence.

The girl peeked around the lilies and bobbed a curtsy. "Good mornin', miss."

Amanda read the questions in the maid's wide brown eyes. Why had she arrived so early in the season? Why in the middle of the night?

Amanda nodded and strolled through the main hall. Sightless eyes of white marble busts and statues stared at her, and she hurried past into the solarium. The orchid Wesley had given her sat in full sun amid potted palms and hibiscus plants. She grunted and moved it to a place where it would receive indirect light. The beautiful flowers that typically cheered her made a lump form in her throat.

Their footman, dressed in livery, held open the French doors to the loggia, and she instructed him to fetch her bow and arrows and arrange a target in the grassy side yard. A gentle sea breeze laced with the scent of salt and honeysuckle swirled around her, and she paused, placing a gloved hand on the pillar of the archway leading down the stone steps, to take in the vaguely familiar scene. The once-tall grass she used to run through was now a tightly manicured lawn, and the stone stairway leading to the ocean now had a walled gate to keep out the commoners who strolled the cliff walk. A bubbling fountain stood off the portico with a view of the vast ocean beyond the stone wall. Deep-blue hydrangeas flowered near the bottom of the steps. Their dainty, lace-capped flowers had just started to bloom, delighting in the sun and humid sea air.

The beauty of the view only prodded her to move along. Such splendor demanded an emotional response, and she stuffed any feelings deep into the recessed area of her mind where she locked away memories of her mother—and now Wesley.

Another footman opened her archery box on a stone bench while the gardener positioned the target. A large beech tree shaded her from the sun, and she practiced pulling back the bow string without an arrow. Tension resisted and strained against her fingers, but she would master it. Life defied and flouted her hopes and dreams, but on the archery field, she was in control, and the arrow would go where she sent it.

"Would you care for some lemonade, miss?"

At her nod, the footman retreated, and she notched

an arrow to her longbow. She raised the string and three fingers to below her left eye, exhaled, and let the arrow fly. It sliced through the air and thumped into the target just below the bullseye. She adjusted and notched another arrow, staying consistent in her movements until the arrows hit the mark. If only her life could have remained as steady.

Other than with the Shoemakers, Lily's family, Wesley had been the only one with whom she could be herself. He had called out her fear of social situations the night they were introduced at the Weathersby ball. Instead of teasing or scoffing, he'd become her white knight, charging into conversations and rescuing her from social humiliation. How would she survive social engagements without him? How would she not embarrass herself and disappoint her father? How would she piece her heart back together?

Her arrow missed the mark and landed in the grass.

She winced and closed her eyes. Pulling another arrow from her quiver, she set it to her bow.

"I've never seen you miss a target."

Her eyes sprung open.

Wesley.

Amanda whirled around with her arrow notched.

*W*esley raised both palms in surrender and backed up a step. "Whoa."

Her stance showed her anger and rightfully so.

But while he had hidden here in wait among the branches of the weeping beech tree, all he had pictured was her in the carriage yesterday with her hand pressed to the window and her expression filled with anguish. She'd displayed that same countenance while pulling back the bow a moment earlier. Sadness had hollowed those beautiful eyes. She'd missed her mark and he'd reacted.

Amanda's mouth struggled to form words. Her chest heaved, and her face contorted in rage until her eyes welled with tears.

"I know you're upset."

Her brow furrowed and then softened. The amber color of her eyes glittered as she blinked back tears, and her gaze hardened, eyebrows snapping together. If she hadn't looked so enchantingly beautiful with her high color and lips so kissable, he might have chuckled at the movement of her eyebrows wiggling like crawling inchworms with each change of expression.

"You followed me to Newport?"

Was that relief? Did he detect a flicker of hopefulness in her eyes?

He could work with that.

"You"—her pitch lowered to a growl—"followed me to Newport."

"Please, I need you to hear my side of what happened." He eyed her tentative hold on the bow string. "I can't avoid scandal. People assume the worst and rake up everything." He stepped away from the arrow's dead-center aim on his heart. "The other night was not what people have deemed."

"You were alone with a woman in your office in the middle of the night. She's claiming she thought you loved her." Amanda's eyes grew glassy and wild, and she jerked up on her bow. "People are drooling over the whole sordid affair, saying you pushed her—tried to kill her off because she was with child, or there was a tussle on the stairs because you told her your plans to marry me."

The rumors were worse than he imagined. His stomach soured as if he'd eaten bad caviar. "I fell asleep in my office going over paperwork. I woke to a scream and a thud and found a woman lying at the bottom of the stairs." He stepped toward her. "Please believe me. I don't know who she is. I've never seen the woman in my life."

"Don't lie to me," Amanda said through clenched teeth. "Her name is Cynthia Blunt. She was at the Simpson's gala. We were both there."

Blunt. His gaze dropped as he tried to reconjure that night.

Amanda sighed and lowered her bow. "The green lowcut dress that hovered near the card tables. I believe she danced with your brother toward the end of the evening."

"Theo had partaken of right much to drink." An image of his brother jawing near the stairs with some brunette wearing rouged lips collided with the memory of the rouge smeared woman being carried by stretcher and grabbing his shirt collar.

He raised his hand and rapidly snapped his fingers. "Wait. I remember her. Lots of lip rouge?"

Amanda issued him a curt nod.

He shook his index finger in the air and shoved his other hand in his pocket as he paced. "Odd laugh—high pitched and nasal. How did she get in the Jansen and Sons office?"

"What were you doing at work so late at night with her?" Amanda's lips thinned.

"I told you. I had some paperwork to read and sign, and I fell asleep."

"How did she get in?"

"I don't know." He gripped his head. "Someone had to let her in, but few people have the key. Theo, myself, a few key staff, and the janitor, I suppose." He closed his eyes and struggled to remember the sound of retreating footfalls and the back door banging. "Someone else had been at the office. I heard footsteps and a door slam."

She blinked, and her angry glint washed into clouded confusion.

Wesley closed the distance between them until the point of her arrow jabbed his thigh. He grasped her shoulders. "I would never hurt you like this. Tell me you believe me."

Her lower lip trembled. "I want to believe you."

"You can." He cupped her face. "You know me. You know my character. I might have been a young blood once, but then I met you."

She closed her eyes, and tears leaked from the corners.

"Darling, look at me."

She squeezed her lids tighter, and a sob tore from her throat.

The sound ripped a hole in his gut. "Please Amanda, look at me." He stroked her cheek with his thumb. "Mandi Mae."

Her eyes opened, and two liquid pools of amber peered at him beneath damp eyelashes.

"I love you. The agreement I was signing the night before last was from your father. I'd come from getting his blessing to ask for your hand."

Her eyes widened the tiniest bit.

"I handled your father's every objection and committed to every stipulation. He drives a hard bargain, but you're worth it. Believe me, no other woman was on my mind that night—only you."

She tried to dip her chin, but he caught it with his curved index finger and lifted until she met his gaze. "No other woman has even crossed my mind since the night you stared me down at the Weathersby party."

"I did nothing of the sort. It's impolite to stare."

He grinned. She was so easy to provoke. It was one of the many things he loved about her. "You didn't watch me from across the room? Admiring the regal way in which I stood, observing the crowd as if patiently enduring their presence? It wasn't you who begged Olivia to help you make my acquaintance?"

"Hardly. You know I was petrified."

"That's right. It was the other way around, me admiring you and pleading with your friend to introduce us." His smile fell. "To everyone else, you looked elegant and bored, but there was a wideness to your eyes and a tightness in the way you clasped your hands that awakened the-knight-in-shining-armor within me. You were a damsel in distress, but I needed to know you more than you needed my aid."

~

*A*manda remembered that night in vivid detail. Wesley had peered at her in a similar fashion as he looked at her now, as if victory was the only acceptable outcome. Her hands had shaken much the same, and the same waves of chills had tingled her skin. Was he friend or foe? Lifeline or anchor sinking her in the deep?

Amanda's father had dragged her to the Weathersby party and promptly left her after spying a business associate. She'd strolled the perimeter of the room, her palms sweating through her gloves. Jewels had sparkled on earlobes, wrists, and chests above lowcut bodices. Colorful silken, lace, and satin flounces, layered like tiered cakes, adorned ladies who peeked around men in black tuxes as they swept across the dance floor.

And a man on the opposite side of the room had boldly held her gaze...

Amanda's throat tightened.

Please don't approach hoping to converse.

Amanda lengthened her stride as much as she could without drawing censure and fled in proper fashion to a safe corner nook. A footman offered her a glass of champagne. She accepted the fluted glass for something to hold but didn't dare swallow the bubbly drink for fear her jittery stomach would revolt.

Away from the hubbub, Amanda slowed her breathing and pretended to sip from her glass. Her father insisted she master her childish nerves, and the best way was to be thrown into the mix. He wouldn't listen regarding how her hands would shake and her tongue would refuse to form proper sentences. She longed to be back with Lily in the Shoemaker's kitchen, baking rolls for supper or sitting in their family's salon while Lily's exuberant voice read to the family. If only she could speak to the fashionable set with the eloquence Lily read Shakespeare.

A nearby bookshelf caught Amanda's eye, and she scanned the authors, Dickens, Thackeray, Ruskin... Oh,

Ruskin's third volume, *Modern Painters.* Her fingers reached for the book, merely to peek.

"Well, halloo, Amanda." Olivia's hand hooked through a man's arm, drawing him in Amanda's direction.

She jerked her arm back to her side, swishing against her London-made liberty silk gown.

It was the man from across the room. His charismatic grin and casual stance with one thumb hooked into his pocket almost made him appear approachable, but Amanda backed up a step, the heel of her shoe colliding with the bookshelf.

Cornered.

"Amanda, darling." Olivia flashed her a smile. "Everyone believes you to be so high in the instep that you'd prefer to stand alone rather than be in the company of bores, but you must be more social."

"I—um—"

Olivia gestured to the man. "Meet Mr. Wesley Jansen, brother of Mr. Theodore Jansen of Jansen and Sons. He has been longing to make your acquaintance." She turned to Mr. Jansen. "Mr. Jansen, this is my dear friend, Amanda Klein, daughter of William Klein."

His bold gaze held hers with a determined twinkle similar to that of her father's after a neat stroke of business. He bowed over her hand. "It is a pleasure, Miss Klein."

Olivia elbowed Mr. Jansen. "There's Mr. Van Hassel

now. Wave him over. I have set my sights on marrying him, so pretend to be paired."

A half smile curved Mr. Jansen's lips, and he had the audacity to wink at Amanda before beckoning Mr. Van Hassel over.

Amanda's gaze drifted to the bookshelf as the trio made introductions and small talk. Mr. Jansen extricated himself from Olivia and Mr. Van Hassel, who were enraptured in the rumors of Alva Vanderbilt divorcing her husband, William.

Mr. Jansen's scent of suede and cedarwood billowed around her like cigar smoke, announcing his nearness. "Which book had you been reaching for earlier?"

Amanda's breath caught. "You were watching me?"

"I couldn't help myself." He shrugged. "You're most intriguing. My guess was Thackeray's *Vanity Fair*."

Intriguing sounded aloof and interesting, and she was neither. "Vanity Fair? The novel without a hero?"

"I haven't read it myself, but I've listened to those who have. It seemed fitting with you standing here observing the idleness and frivolity of New York's fashionable set as if above their antics. An angel on a pedestal whose perfection cannot be equaled by those who attempt to reach to her heights."

An inelegant snort escaped her nose at his absurd assumption. "You are far off the mark, Mr. Jansen. I'd been reaching for Ruskin's book."

"Ah, an enthusiast of the arts? Do you paint?"

"I'm afraid I lack the talent, but I admire the beauty of it."

His expression turned earnest, and his intense gaze held hers as if reading into her past and her future.

The bookshelf opened behind them, and Amanda startled.

"I beg your pardon." Mr. Charles Weathersby stepped out of the hidden entrance carrying a crystal decanter of amber liquid and several glasses.

"What's the occasion, Weathersby?" Mr. Jansen stepped aside to let their robust host with a mutton chop beard pass.

"A toast to a lucky turn. I gambled on a short, and it paid out a bundle."

"You bet against a stock?" Mr. Van Hassel perked up.

"Indeed. I'll tell you about it in the billiard room if you want a drop of the good stuff to celebrate." He pushed the bookshelf closed with his elbow, and Amanda felt a tug on the train of her gown.

Mr. Weathersby sauntered past, and Mr. Van Hassel hooked Olivia's arm. "You don't have to ask us twice. Lead on, Weathersby. We're ready to celebrate."

Amanda discreetly yanked on her bustle. It didn't budge. Her gown had caught in the door. If others discovered her predicament, all eyes would be on her. She clasped her hands at her waist to keep them from trembling.

Mr. Jansen held out his elbow. "Would you care to follow them?"

"I think not." She pasted a demure smile on her lips. "I'm content here for the moment."

"Very well."

When he didn't excuse himself to join his friends, Amanda pretended to sip from her glass. Why wouldn't he leave? She must think of a way to extricate herself from the bookcase, not focus on small talk.

"Would you care to dance?"

She loved dancing. "Perhaps another time."

"A stroll along the terrace while the weather holds?"

"Thank you, but no."

He grabbed two full champagne glasses off a passing tray and held one out to her.

"Thank you, but as you can see"—she held up her glass—"I already have one."

"I figured you may prefer a different kind, since you've pretended to drink from that same glass for the past twenty minutes." He removed the warm champagne from her gloved hand and set it on a nearby end table, trading it for the chilled glass.

"That's wholly unnecessary."

He turned to stand shoulder to shoulder and watch the crowd. "It may bolster your courage."

"Courage?"

"To tell me you're stuck."

The blood drained from her face, cooling her warm cheeks.

"How long were you planning to stand here with

your gown caught in the bookcase?" He raised his hand and signaled a servant.

She gripped his wrist and pulled his arm down, too late, for a servant ran over to do his bidding.

Mr. Jansen peered at her. Concern darkened his gaze.

Dear Lord, he must have felt her shaking. She released his wrist and swallowed to find her voice. "Please don't make a scene."

He stepped forward and whispered in the servant's ear.

The servant's gaze lowered to the hem of her gown, and he nodded. "Right away, sir." The man scurried off.

"So what is it that you love about art?"

As Amanda responded, Wesley engaged her in topics she enjoyed, and to her surprise, their conversation deepened to what made something beautiful beyond a superficial veneer and how the character within defined a person, topics Lily, her governess, had loved to discuss, and in turn, Amanda too.

Several full sets of music passed, and the orchestra stopped for an intermission. When had the hour grown so late? She blinked at the gentleman beside her. How had she conversed this easily with Mr. Jansen? Did he find her interesting? She rejected the notion. He probably stayed to be polite due to her predicament.

"I don't mean to ruin your evening." Amanda sipped from her glass. "You mustn't feel the need to stay by my side."

"Ruin? This has been the most enjoyable evening I've had in some time." The jaunty grin returned to his lips. "Besides, what kind of gentleman would I be if I left a damsel in distress to her own ends?"

The servant returned and apologized for taking so long to find the key. He lifted a false volume of the *Odyssey,* and Wesley moved to stand in front of the servant so no one would take note.

The taut pull of her bustle fell slack, and she stepped forward.

"Freed from bondage at last." He held up his elbow. "Shall we see where the evening takes us?"

She glanced at New York's inner sanctum of high society, flitting about, exuding their wealth and power to align with others a step or two above them. Amanda's breathing quickened. She hesitated, having enjoyed the haven of their isolation and private one-on-one conversation.

"What are you afraid of?" He squeezed her hand as if to reassure her. "Surely, you know no one in this room holds a candle to you?"

"It's..." She shook her head. They'd only just met. She shouldn't confide her inadequacies, but the open way he peered at her, as if he already knew but patiently waited for her to speak, drew it from her lips. "I struggle with idle chatter and fear people will find me dull."

"Miss Klein, I can assure you, you are anything but a bore." He tucked her hand into the crook of his arm.

"Stay by my side. I will show you how it's done, for this is something in which I excel."

Her expression must have shown her fright, for he chuckled before guiding her to a group of the younger set and struck up a conversation about which opera house was better, the Metropolitan or the Academy of Music…

Mr. Wesley Jansen had proved to be a master at his craft, and even though Amanda had said little that evening, she'd been deemed a success. Invitations poured in for her attendance at additional events, much to her horror.

But Wesley had been there at the next soiree and the following party and saw her through until she almost looked forward to such events, if only to see him.

Now he stood before her, the intensity of his gray eyes pleading for understanding. How could she walk away when he'd been there for her? How could she believe the worst when he'd shown her nothing but devotion? Was her fear of scandal and unwanted attention distorting her view?

"I know you're afraid." His fingertips trailed the line of her jaw, and his gaze dropped for the briefest of moments to her lips.

She swallowed, longing to feel the power of his mouth move over hers, melt away her fears, sooth her like a balm.

"You suffered because of your mother. If I could take this away, I would, but we can face it together. I will be by your side and you by mine. I'll find a way to prove my devotion and clear my reputation." He cupped her chin with the curve of his index finger. "Just say you'll give me the chance."

Behind the shrubbery, ice cubes clanked against the sides of a glass pitcher.

"Hang it. The footman's returning. I must go." Desperation showed in Wesley's eyes, but he didn't move. He risked being caught, waiting for her answer.

God, what should I do?

She nodded. It was slight. If he hadn't been holding her chin, he might not have known she agreed, but his quick smile confirmed he did.

He gripped her shoulders and brushed his lips across hers in a brief kiss. "Friday night, come to the Hagen party, but refuse to dance with me."

Refuse him? Why? She furrowed her brow.

"Just until the gossip has died down, then you take me back out of the goodness of your heart." One foot shifted to turn away, but he hesitated.

The clanking of ice cubes grew closer, and she glimpsed a tray floating above the top of the trimmed hedge. The footman neared the entrance.

Wesley crushed her to him, his fingers digging into her back and his lips searing hers with a final kiss. And then he was gone, disappearing into the cover of the weeping beech tree branches. Her lips tingled, and she touched her mouth where she'd been kissed as heat rose into her cheeks. Her arrow lay on the grass, and her bow dangled from her other hand.

The footman set the tray on a stand and passed her a lemonade. She gulped it down in an unladylike fashion to cool her burning body.

Would the mere sight of them together stir up a scandal?

Could Wesley's love sustain her through the trial of her greatest fear?

CHAPTER 5

*C*alling cards and invitations poured in over the next few days as summer guests arrived at their cottages earlier than prior summers. Aunt Sally stood in the doorway of the solarium and waved the coveted invitations in excitement, only to frown. "You don't think we've become the thing because our friends desire new gossip?"

Amanda spritzed her orchid with water. Without Wesley as her strong pillar to lean on, she'd best avoid social situations, at least until the Hagen party. Amanda passed the spray bottle to a footman and wandered into the Rosewood Salon. She picked up an Ouida novel to take her mind off the present and sat on the settee to read.

Aunt Sally swept into the room after her, still frowning. "You must change, my dear. It's our at-home-day to accept callers."

Why did she have to change clothing for every occasion? If Aunt Sally knew she used to wear the same dress for an entire day—sometimes two days straight—she'd probably faint. "I won't be receiving callers this afternoon. I've already informed Calvin."

"Calvin?"

"The butler."

"Oh, yes. Right." Aunt Sally raised her bustle and perched on the sofa, arranging her skirts. "I don't understand why you won't visit with people. Wouldn't it be best to let the gossipmongers know you're cutting all ties to Mr. Jansen? Then we can socialize and enjoy summering in Newport."

Aunt Sally had never understood the swirling stomach, faint sheen of sweat, and thickness of tongue that affected her niece during social engagements. Her aunt, like Amanda's father, had always brushed it off as a silly nuance Amanda would outgrow.

"It's a good thing I'm not a mere caller." Olivia strode into the room with her agreeable husband, Jeffrey, trotting behind.

Amanda set her book aside and rose.

"I came as fast as I could. I knew you'd need my backing through the horrid scandal Mr. Jansen created." Olivia gripped Amanda's elbows and kissed the air on either side of her cheeks. She whispered in Amanda's ear, "Did I see Mr. Jansen leaving on horseback?"

Amanda gasped but tried to recover. "He wouldn't dare."

Olivia pulled back. "I heard Miss Blunt is recovering at her home but has gone strangely silent." Olivia greeted Aunt Sally before lifting her bustle and settling onto the sofa. "Jeffrey, darling, come sit." She patted the cushion next to her.

Jeffrey bowed stiffly to Amanda and Aunt Sally before dropping onto the couch next to his wife. He shifted in his seat and gripped a decorative pillow, hugging it against his side.

"Calvin, have tea and finger sandwiches brought immediately." Aunt Sally perched on the edge of a chair.

Jeffrey cleared his throat. "Mind if I have something a bit stronger?"

"Certainly." Aunt Sally gestured to the crystal decanter on the side table.

He rose, poured himself a glass of amber liquid, and returned to the couch.

"I can't believe you must endure this again." Olivia clicked her tongue. "It's as bad as your mother's scandal, with people crawling all over to hear the details."

Aunt Sally pressed her hands to her cheeks. "Upon my soul, that was dreadful. We had no choice but to ship Amanda off with her governess after we found people eavesdropping from the child's balcony." She pressed a hand to her heart. "Her mother, Cora, was as lovely as a flower garden but had lavish impulses. Her dramatic accusations that William held her prisoner before she ran off with Captain Adams and William's yacht was outrageous, to say the least. William had to deal with numerous inquisitions, accusations, loss of business dealings, his wife's affair, and her death." She sighed. "It was too much for one soul to bear, but he managed."

"This time, Amanda can't be sent to live in obscurity." Olivia sent her a sympathetic look. "We'll figure a way out of this mess. You can give that vulture the cut direct at the Hagen party or an intentional slight every time he requests a dance. I saw the invitation sitting in your correspondence tray."

"A capital idea, my dear." Aunt Sally nodded sagely.

Olivia pointed her finger at Amanda. "Don't even think about declining. You must accept. By the end of the night, he'll be begging for a smidgeon of your attention, and a public snub will serve that blooming bounder right for what he did. You'll show our set that his affections had already grown tiresome." She leaned forward. "I know just what to do. I'll introduce you to that handsome libertine, Mr. Carter. You can let Mr. Jansen think you've already moved on."

Amanda shook her head. "I couldn't—"

"Fiddlesticks." Olivia pursed her lips. "Of course, you can. All along, I've known you could do better than Jansen. Mr. Carter is from old money, and old money is far better than new money. Mr. Jansen's luck could turn, and we all know that the old money sustains."

Outside, carriage wheels crunched on gravel.

Aunt Sally twisted in her seat to peek out the window. "It's your father."

Amanda stiffened. He must have heard the rumors because he rarely came to Newport during the work week.

The room fell silent as his footfalls approached the house. The front door opened, and the butler welcomed Mr. Klein back to Breakwater Court.

Her father grunted and called for Sally.

"In here, William," Her aunt answered.

"You tell Amanda that Jansen's cut off." His clipped steps slapped the marble floors.

Jeffrey straightened to attention.

"There will be no merger and no marriage after what that nitwit pulled." Her father stopped in the doorway, his normal stern expression darkening. "You have company."

"Surely the Van Hassels are considered family after all Olivia has done for Amanda." Aunt Sally rose and greeted her brother with a kiss to his cheek.

"Good afternoon, Mr. Klein." Olivia nodded to Amanda's father. "We don't mean to put you out. We'll be on our way shortly. I merely hoped to check on Amanda's wellbeing after"—she grimaced—"everything that happened."

Amanda's stomach sank, but she forced the quiver from her voice. "Good afternoon, father."

The corners of his lips turned down as if regretting his earlier outburst. "I know you fancied that b'hoy, but

I want you to put him from your mind. We should be the ones riding him out on a rail, not the other way around."

"Hear, hear, sir." Jeffrey raised his glass.

"Pour me one of those." Her father gestured to Jeffrey's glass and leaned against the fireplace mantel.

Jeffrey rushed to comply. The potent smell of scotch assaulted Amanda's senses as he handed it to her father.

Her father tossed back a gulp and pointed to her with his glass. "He thinks he bested some old coot, but I'll show him. I'll sink him and Jansen and Sons along with him."

Amanda squeezed the fingers of one hand so hard, the tips turned purple. Did Wesley know what he was up against? Should she warn him?

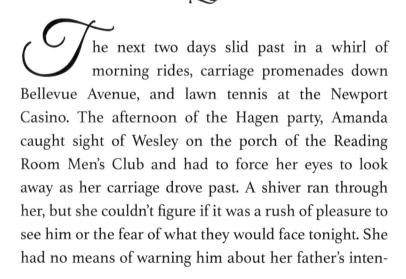

The next two days slid past in a whirl of morning rides, carriage promenades down Bellevue Avenue, and lawn tennis at the Newport Casino. The afternoon of the Hagen party, Amanda caught sight of Wesley on the porch of the Reading Room Men's Club and had to force her eyes to look away as her carriage drove past. A shiver ran through her, but she couldn't figure if it was a rush of pleasure to see him or the fear of what they would face tonight. She had no means of warning him about her father's intensions—not without creating gossip that would get back to her father's ears.

Afternoon fell into evening, and Amanda picked the Hagen invitation off her dressing room table. "Ladies are to wear red." She tossed the invite down. "Red is a strange request for this time of year. I could see it more for Christmas or Valentine's Day." She turned her back for Katie to tighten her corset.

"I've heard Mamie Fish has had stranger requests for her parties." Katie tugged on the strings, stealing Amanda's breath for a moment. "I heard she once threw a dinner party on horseback."

"I wasn't able to attend that one, but many guests commented on it." Conversations were minimal as partygoers ate and clung to their horses. She might have enjoyed the event. Amanda ducked her head as Katie guided the dress over her, and Amanda poked her arms into the sleeves. "Thankfully, a red gown was packed."

Katie hooked the back of the dress. "Have you heard about those new zipper contraptions? I fear they might run me out of a job." She snickered. "But I bet young bloods will be paying homage to the Universal Fastener Company for making their indiscretions easier."

Amanda's gaze flew to the maid, and Katie had the wherewithal to blush. "Pardon, miss. I forgot myself and spoke out of turn."

"How do I look?" Amanda turned, which heightened the fluttering of her stomach.

Katie paused, but her gaze fell away. "Lovely, Miss Klein."

"You don't like it."

"What's not to like?" She folded the discarded clothing. "The gown is gorgeous."

"What's wrong with it?" She hesitated but then squeezed Katie's hand. In the last few days, they'd shared confidences, and Amanda felt as though she'd found a friend. "Tell me the truth."

"The ruling clans don't want to hear a maid's opinion. I've seen it. They befriend their servants, but as soon as they say something that doesn't tickle their ears, the maid is tossed out on her backside. We're disposable, and I need this job. My boyfriend and I are saving to get married."

"I'm not going to terminate your employment because of your opinion, and I may look like a New York knickerbocker, but I spent most of my life in a two-room house in northern Virginia."

Katie set fisted hands on her hips and smiled. "I knew you were different."

"In a good way, I hope."

Katie winked at her. "Of course. At least, to us servants."

"Then tell me what's wrong with the gown. I need tonight to go smoothly."

"Honestly?" Katie stepped back and gripped her chin. "With the leg-of-mutton sleeves and the hourglass waist, you look like a heart."

Amanda turned to the mirror. Katie was right. "Oh dear." She gulped. "What should I do?"

"I can make some alterations. In the winters, I work as a seamstress, but will you trust me with some daring fashion trends?"

Amanda pressed a hand to her stomach and nodded. "But please keep in mind, I want to blend in, not stand out."

CHAPTER 6

*A*manda tried not to grip her father's arm too tightly as they alighted from the carriage. Katie followed behind in case Amanda's dress needed tending, but Aunt Sally had eaten something that disagreed with her and at the last minute decided not to attend the Hagen party. Aunt Sally's indecision on whether or not to accompany them had set their arrival past fashionably late. Amanda worked to keep her breathing at a steady rhythm because she'd have no choice but to make a grand entrance at this hour.

Father handed the butler their invitation, and the doors were swung wide.

Amanda ran her hand down the sleek, no-frills gown Katie had altered. Gone were the mutton sleeves, replaced with tiny caps. The waist narrowed into a *V* in front, and the bustle remained, but the only decoration was a black lace ruffle on the bottom and a black lace tulle tucker to hide her cleavage. Her throat tightened. The gown's simplicity alone would cause her to stand out.

She gripped the curved marble railing, and her father hauled her up the six red-carpeted stairs to the ballroom. Her gown's short train trailed behind. Laughter and music bounced off the high coffered ceilings and wainscoted walls, and a tremor ran through her. How would she manage without Wesley?

Her father halted before the top step.

A sea of white and black whirled before them under the crystal chandeliers, specifically, with the ladies dressed in black or white ball gowns and the men dressed in tuxedos with white shirts and cravats.

Amanda's breathing stilled.

Mrs. Hagen rushed to their side, her face pale and made even more so by her black lace gown. "Mr. and Miss Klein. How lovely to see you. Did you not read the invitation? It's a black-and-white party." She gestured to the guests. "I thought it might be fun—like an image from a daguerreotype come to life."

Amanda's father yanked the invitation from his pocket and flipped it open. "It says no such thing."

Mrs. Hagen scanned the contents and paled whiter than the gentlemen's shirtfronts. "Oh dear. I extended you an invitation, but this isn't the one I sent. It's not my handwriting."

The ballroom quieted, and eyes riveted in their direction.

Amanda swayed on her feet.

Her father tensed and pulled her up the last stair. "You must pull this off. Jansen is trying to make a laughingstock out of the Klein name." Her father's low growl rumbled through Amanda.

Her lips parted to defend Wesley, but no words passed through her constricted chest and throat.

"I'm getting a drink." He strode toward the card room.

He left her.

Her feet numbed, and she stared at his retreating form as whispers grew with the occasional snort of laughter. *Ruined the Klein name. So distasteful. Cora Klein is a disgrace.* Voices from the past burst out of the trunk she'd locked and then tossed away the key.

A hand pressed into her back. "Miss? How about we bustle the dress so you might dance?"

Katie.

"The retiring room is past the ballroom, down the hall on the right." Mrs. Hagen stepped aside for them to pass.

The pressure on Amanda's lower back increased until her numb toes had no choice but to move. "That's it, miss," Katie whispered. "Chin high."

Guests parted as she passed, their lips twisting into mocking smiles or opening in shocked gasps. The orchestra played a soft tune on the balcony, but Amanda heard Beethoven's Fifth Symphony of pending doom.

A couple of gentlemen stepped out of the library. Their laughing discussion died. Wesley's gaze locked on her. Admiration lit his face, until his gaze skittered over the black-and-white crowd and back to her red gown. His eyes widened.

Dizziness washed over her.

Katie gripped her elbow. "This way, miss." She guided her into a hall, pushed her though the door to the retiring room, and lowered her into a chair. Katie squatted beside her and fanned Amanda with her apron. "You did great. The worst is over."

Olivia burst into the retiring room. "How did this happen? What a disaster." She yanked Katie up by her arm and spun the maid to face her. "You must go at once and get her a black gown."

"But they've seen the red dress," Katie said. "They'll know she knuckled under."

Olivia released Katie as if she were a filthy rag. "What do you know about the fashionable set?"

"Katie and my father are right." Amanda stood and rubbed her temples. "I must pull this off."

Olivia placed a comforting arm around Amanda's shoulders. "She doesn't know what you've been through. It'll be too much."

"I'm just the help." Katie knelt at Amanda's feet, bustling her gown's train. "But I've handled my share of bullies. You can't let them see weakness. They'll only attack you harder."

"We don't require a servant's advice." Olivia shooed Katie with her hand.

"No." Amanda gripped Katie's sleeve. "Please, continue."

Katie hesitated. "You can deter them a few ways—by a force of strength, making light of the situation, or taking them by surprise."

Olivia snorted.

"You're a rose blooming in a thistle garden." Katie smiled. "Show them not just the beauty on the outside but surprise them by what's on your inside. My mama always says, 'a little sugar makes bitter tea easier to drink.'"

"Rubbish." Olivia shook her head. "It would be social suicide. You'd be better off sneaking out the back and giving everyone the slip. I'll tell everyone you weren't well."

Amanda pushed to her feet and peered at herself in the looking glass. Was she strong enough to face her fear? Her governess's voice rang in her head. *Bloom where you're planted because God has tilled the soil.* Amanda nodded to Katie and spoke the words before she lost her nerve. "Let's finish bustling this gown."

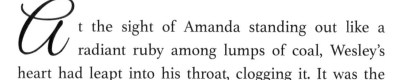

t the sight of Amanda standing out like a radiant ruby among lumps of coal, Wesley's heart had leapt into his throat, clogging it. It was the first time in his life he'd been at a loss of words. The man he'd been pitching the new petroleum engine fuel to had elbowed him and said, "Isn't that Miss Klein, the woman you fancied?"

Amanda had looked stunning and woefully frightened at the same time as her maid accompanied her to the retiring room, but why did she wear a red dress to a black-and-white party? She hated attention.

Wesley had itched to climb over the crowd and block her from their sight. He had to help her through this debacle, but the plan was for her to refuse him and then find it in her generous heart to take him back after the scandal died. Eventually, all would be forgotten, and life could return to normal, but this fiasco would only rake up further gossip. There must be a way to turn this around. He needed to convince the crowd that this was intentional.

"I still fancy her." His voice cracked, but at least it had returned. "For a moment, I thought she was a figment of my imagination." He elbowed the man. "I'm glad you saw her too. What an entrance. Exquisite. I've got to get in line for that first dance."

"Capital idea."

One of the boys from the club clasped a hand on his shoulder. "I guarantee some maid is going to be fired over that mistake."

"Or given a hefty raise. What a better way to show Miss Klein's unique beauty?" Wesley slapped the back of his hand to the man's chest. "Miss Klein is the matador's cape, and we are the bulls, my friend. Get prepared, because she's just toying with us."

Wesley held back his smile as his friend leaned toward Miss Jasper on his arm, who held a propensity to gossip. She, in turn, whispered behind her palm frond fan to her gathered brood of hens.

In a matter of minutes, the room buzzed with sentiments of how this had all been planned to set the tone of the summer galas. And what a better person to set the stage than the one all the talk was about.

"It's like a second coming out," Wesley overheard one guest say.

"I think red is about to be all the rage," said another.

The cluster of guests inched their way closer to the hall leading to the retiring rooms. Women raised onto their toes, and men craned their necks for the view of Miss Klein's return.

"Is it true Miss Klein is accepting attentions?" A fellow nudged Wesley's arm.

"Not if I can change her mind." Wesley glared at the man to intimidate him. "And stand back, because I plan to do it." He edged in front of the bloke.

The final phase of his original plan was for him to come across as the repentant fool. No one would believe the truth of his falling asleep at Jansen and Sons and waking to a woman's scream. He had no witnesses, and it sounded unbelievable even in his own mind, but if he could manipulate the rumors, he and Amanda could move past this quicker. If she danced with him and took him back right away, she'd come off as desperate or hard put. But if she initially snubbed him and he made it look as though she begrudgingly accepted him back, then she'd be cast in a good light, and he'd be considered a bloomin' bounder who'd come around after realizing the error of his ways.

Giddiness welled in his chest. If all went swimmingly, he might be able to propose to Amanda by the end of the week. The only hang up was that his plan tarnished his reputation, and her father would not be pleased.

A blast of chilled air drew his gaze to the French doors leading to the veranda. Standing in the opening, Mr. Klein clenched the end of his cigar between his teeth and glared at Wesley through narrowed eyes.

Wesley swallowed around his tight collar. Maybe his proposal would need a couple of weeks.

A flash of red had all faces swiveling in that direction. Mrs. Van Hassel entered the ballroom first and scurried to her husband's side. Amanda stopped on the threshold.

She stood regal like a queen, surveying the crowd from under her dark, sweeping lashes. Every muscle in Wesley's body tightened with the urge to pull her into his arms. Crowd be hanged. Unlike the other ladies in the room who bedecked themselves in ostentatious jewels, Amanda wore small diamond teardrop earrings and a tasteful diamond pendant necklace that rested just below her exposed collarbones.

Above the diamond pendant, the dip of that graceful alcove at the base of her neck deepened as she struggled to breathe.

She was frightened out of her mind.

Her gaze found his. Relief flashed in those amber eyes, and her chest rose in a deep breath.

His heart pounded against his breastbone. *Do something,* his mind screamed. *Help her, you fool.* Sweat broke across his brow, but he willed his feet to remain in place. With his eyes, he pleaded for her to understand and remember what he'd said at the archery field. His toes curled in his shoes, and it pained him to shake his head—a slight shake only Amanda would notice.

She paled and ever-so-slightly nodded before her gaze flicked away.

Thank heaven she could read him like no other. Just one of the other many things he loved about her. Now was his chance. He strode forward and donned the same smile he used to win over hearts and business contracts.

"Miss Klein, may I say, you look smashing in red. Would you care to dance?"

Her gaze met his, and hesitation flashed in those amber depths.

He offered what he hoped was an almost imperceivable nod to encourage her.

The cords of her neck tightened as she swallowed, but she lifted her chin and peered down her regal nose at him. "It's poorly done of you, Mr. Jansen, to ask for the first dance after the spectacle you put me through. It shall take some wheedling to get back into my good graces."

His chest swelled with a silent *hurrah* at her display of courage, but he kept his composure. "I'm grateful for the opportunity and will endeavor with all my being to fall back into your favor." He bowed low before her as a sign of humility and backed away.

Before he could turn, the young bloods swooped in to be the first to dance with the belle of the party. One over-excited fellow accidentally elbowed Wesley in the ribs trying to press to the front of the line. Several people stepped on Wesley's toes as he was forced to the periphery of the crowd.

One randy philanderer after another led Amanda onto the dance floor. She did a thumping job of showing each partner the barest of interest, enough for them to drool after her, but not enough to lead them to believe she'd entertain their pursuit. Her neck and shoulders remained tight, but dancing was the perfect way for her to pass the time because it didn't require much conversation.

Wesley leaned against a Roman column, accepted a drink from a passing servant, and observed her. Pretending to sulk in a jealous manner wasn't difficult, for his gaze fell to young Mr. Swendle's hand sliding lower on her back, and he considered breaking the man's fingers. And earlier when his old classmate, Jack

Downing, held her a tad too close, Wesley envisioned fixing the lad's flint by rearranging his nose.

"You bungled your opportunity." Jeffrey Van Hassel joined him near the pillar and snorted. "Bully for Miss Klein for pulling this off. Olivia told me there was an invite mishap."

More like treachery. Wesley acknowledged Van Hassel with the lift of his glass and caught sight of his society walker wife, Olivia Van Hassel, attempting to work her way into a conversation with Mrs. Caroline Astor, the high priestess of New York's knickerbockers.

"Mr. Klein looked to pitch a fit when you requested a dance. It might be best if you walked away from his daughter. There are plenty of enchanting ladies within our set to catch a fellow's eye."

"Miss Klein isn't the kind of woman one walks away from."

At least not with his heart intact.

CHAPTER 7

*A*manda was going to retch.

Her stomach heaved when Mr. Swendle led her off the dance floor before the song had finished so they could "jaw for a few moments"—his words. As he drew her to the refreshment table, her mind screamed in protest, *Lord, help me. I can't chitchat. You allowed Aaron to speak for Moses. I need Wesley to speak for me.*

"I'm so pleased to hear you're accepting other attentions." Mr. Swendle paused as if waiting for her to respond.

Her stomach clenched.

"I thought you and Mr. Jansen were headed to the altar."

She pressed a gloved finger to her lips to hold down her nausea and caught sight of Wesley near a pillar. He eyed her as if ready to swoop in if necessary.

"Miss Klein." Mr. Swendle touched her elbow.

She lowered her hand and exhaled slowly. How did Wesley do it? How did he converse so effortlessly with others?

"That was in bad form." Mr. Swendle shook his head and lowered his voice. "I understand it's too early yet to speak of what happened. Forgive my ill manners."

Wesley asked questions. He got them speaking. She'd stood by Wesley's side and witnessed his tactics. He made it look easy. Could she do the same?

You can do all things through Christ who strengthens you.

"Ah, Mr. Swendle." She gripped her hands at her waist to press her stomach back down where it should be. "Um—where did you attend school?"

"Princeton College grad, and while I was boarding there, assistant editor to the *Princetonian* and proud member of their eatery club at the inn."

"Eatery club?" She squeaked the words past the knot in her throat.

"It's a social club with elite members—quite distinguished to be let in."

"Bully for you." *Bully?* She sounded like a young blood. Did ladies use such expressions? Had Olivia ever said such a thing? Merciful heavens, she was making a fool of herself.

"Bully, indeed." He dipped his chin in a salute of sorts. "I say, you'll be at Bailey's beach tomorrow, won't you? All the younger set will be there."

"Pardon me." The little supper she ate refused to stay down. "I must freshen up." She gathered her skirts and strode to the retiring room.

Katie stood as she entered. "May I help you with something, miss?"

Amanda rushed to the water closet and vomited.

"Oh, Miss Klein." Katie handed her a rag to wipe her mouth. "You must not have a stomach for drink."

"It's nerves." She wiped her mouth. "My stomach can't handle talking to people."

Katie scratched under the brim of her nob cap. "You speak right fine with me."

Amanda rose and stepped out of the water closet, feeling better. She inhaled a deep breath and shook out her hands. She didn't feel the need to retch when speaking to Katie, nor Lily, or Wesley. She had gotten queasy the first few occasions when she spoke to Olivia, but that resolved over time. "I guess it only happens with certain people."

"A wretched curse, I bet." Katie offered a sympathetic frown.

The door swung open. "There you are." Olivia swept into the retiring room. "Mr. Mansfield is looking for you. He says you promised him a dance. People are starting to wonder about your long disappearance."

Truly? Did they have nothing else with which to occupy their minds? "I will be but a moment." She stared at her reflection in the mirror and murmured Scripture.

"Whatever are you muttering?" Olivia pursed her lips.

Amanda straightened and paraphrased a verse from the book of Esther. "Perhaps it's this moment for which I was made."

"Silly. I'm the one who made you." Olivia exited with a sigh. "I'll stall for you."

Katie watched Olivia leave, then flashed Amanda an encouraging smile. "I'll be here if you need me."

"Thank you, Katie." Amanda returned one of her own. "You're a dear."

"Keep your chin high, miss."

She'd have to, if for no other reason than to keep the rising bile in her throat.

~

The hour grew late, and Wesley had properly bid his time. The last notes of the orchestra's set floated over the room, and the musicians stopped for a brief intermission. Wesley raised a finger and flagged down a waiter, asking him to fetch a glass of lemonade. The servant promptly returned with his request.

Mr. Peters, a young fop who grinned like a lovesick simpleton at Amanda, bowed and escorted her off the dance floor. He swiped a pair of champagne glasses off a tray and attempted to press one into Amanda's hand.

"I beg your pardon." Wesley stepped in front of the

lad and passed her the glass of lemonade. "I figured you might be in need of refreshment."

Amanda's eyes softened, and she accepted his glass.

"See here," Peters protested.

Wesley clapped the lad on the shoulder. "Miss Klein doesn't touch spirits, old chap." He pivoted to face Amanda and offered her his arm. "I daresay I owe you some wheedling, so shall we take a turn about the room?"

To his admiration, Amanda sighed and cast her gaze toward the ceiling as if beseeching heaven to get this business with Wesley done and over with.

He tucked her hand into the crook of his arm. "You are getting along capitally." He allowed a smug smile for others to see his delight. The weight of the room's stares followed them as they turned the corner. If the crowd's intense curiosity put Wesley's senses on high alert, he could only imagine what it was doing to Amanda.

"This ruse is taking much out of me." Her steps slowed as if she was weary. "I think Mr. Flannagan felt me tremble, but I led him to believe it was over the steps of the new country dance."

"You must hold up a bit longer. We'll take a turn, get a bit of fresh air on the balcony, and then allow me one dance."

She nodded and leaned a bit more on his arm. "I don't know how this all happened. It's as if someone is playing a terrible prank on me."

"I know the feeling all too well." He held open the

door to the terrace, and refreshing night air cooled his face. A few couples dotted the veranda, holding their own private conversations near potted ferns.

Amanda placed her hands on the railing and peered up at the stars. The moonlight cast her features in black and white.

He joined her, allowing their arms to brush. "We don't have much time, but I needed to make sure your heart is..." His throat constricted, but he choked the words out, needing to know the truth. "Still for me?"

Her head turned so quickly to face him that her small teardrop earrings swung back and forth. She searched his face, and he held his breath. Another thing he loved about her was how she didn't take things lightly and her words were true, but the momentary pause felt like an eternity.

"I've had time to think over what happened in New York. My father confirmed you were with him only a couple hours prior, detailing a marriage agreement. It would make sense that you'd take the paperwork back to your office. It doesn't explain why Miss Blunt was inside Jansen and Sons."

"Yes, a mystery to me as well."

The corners of her lips twitched into a small smile. "But you were willing to sacrifice your pride and social status tonight for my benefit. I overheard some of the rumors, such as I'm the matador's cape, and I'm just toying with you, and you'd sacrifice a year's profits to win me back."

His lips parted. The last one was true—he'd sacrifice even more than that—but he couldn't recall stating it.

"Don't deny you started them." She arched a slender brow, then sighed. "I couldn't have pulled this off alone."

He pretended to fix a loose tendril of her hair, and leaning in, lightly brushed his lips against her smooth cheek. "We're better together," he whispered and heard her quick intake of breath.

"You told me that you didn't know Miss Blunt was in the office, but then you convinced everyone else that you made a terrible mistake letting another turn your head and that you now want me back. Wouldn't the full truth be better?"

"People believe what they want to believe."

"I want to believe you."

There were too many prying eyes for him to pull her behind the potted fern and kiss her properly, and doing so wouldn't create the picture of her reluctantly taking him back. But in that moment, his need to touch her threatened to consume him. He scooped up her gloved hand, pressed the back of it to his cheek, and dropped to one knee like a knight swearing fidelity to his queen.

Amanda's gaze darted to the other couples present.

Miss Jasper halted her male companion, Mr. Bellows. She leaned toward him and whispered behind her fan.

Wesley raised his voice enough for them to overhear. "Amanda, I've been a cad. I will follow you anywhere, to Antarctica and back, if only you'd forgive me and once again take seriously my pursuit of you."

"I-I will take it under consideration." The panicked look returned to her eyes.

He should have prepped her in advance for his performance, but it had been a spontaneous act. He rose and tucked her gloved hand into the crook of his arm. "At least grace me with a dance as you stated you might."

She hesitated.

Mr. Bellows moved to return to the ballroom, but Miss Jasper yanked him back.

Wesley's heartbeat slowed as he waited for Amanda's answer. Should he have stuck with the truth even if it took longer to accomplish the goal?

"Very well." Amanda released an exasperated sigh.

He grinned like a simpleton, but a niggling left him unsettled.

As Wesley escorted her back into the house, Mr. Bellows made eye contact, and the clever fellow pretended to tip his hat in a bully-for-you salute.

Amanda raised her fan and whispered. "Mrs. Hagen said she'd extended me an invitation, but the one I received wasn't in her handwriting. Why would someone tamper with my invite? Why would they derive pleasure from making a fool of me?"

He snorted. "Because the whole lot of them are crabs."

Amanda faltered a step. "Crabs?"

The orchestra returned to their chairs and prepared their sheet music.

Wesley strolled the long way around the room's perimeter to the dance floor. "A couple of summers, I tried my hand at crab fishing for sport. The captain who taught me threw the crabs in a bucket—no lid or anything to keep them inside. I asked if they'd climb out, but the captain laughed and said to watch. As soon as one crab looked as though he was going to make it over the edge to his escape, the other little buggers pulled him back down into the bucket. According to the captain, not a single one had ever gotten away."

The conductor tapped his stick, and the musicians raised their instruments.

"I'm not following." Amanda issued him a sideways glance.

He gestured to the room with his chin before sweeping her into a waltz hold. "These are the crabs, and this gilded inner sanctum is the bucket. If someone gets too high within its walls, others will tear them down." He glided her across the floor. "You'd been hidden away by your father and suddenly returned to the scene. A beautiful woman with the backing of old money threatens their power and control. Your anxious nature toward people is a self-protective measure, for you innately grasp the fickle dispositions of our set."

She moved with him to the triple step as if they'd grown up dancing together, but the tiny crease between her brows showed she still contemplated his crab theory. If she continued to look distraught, he'd not be able to convince others that she'd willingly taken him back. He must get her to laugh or smile or, at the very least, appear content.

"Mandi Mae." He whispered her pet name, and her gaze jumped to his. "If you could go anywhere in the world, where would you go? I should like to take you there."

"Not Antarctica."

Wesley burst with laughter at her clipped tone. Gazes swiveled in their direction.

Her lips curved into a teasing smile. "You were able to make such a vow to follow me to Antarctica and back because you knew I despise the cold and would never willingly travel there."

"True enough. I've never seen a lady bundle herself so thoroughly to walk the snowy streets of New York." He couldn't subdue his wide grin. Great Scott, he adored her wit. "I hope you don't lessen the validity of my vow solely because I erred in my place of reference."

Her expression sobered, and the warm hue of her eyes brightened. "I believe you."

His fingertips reflexively curved into her lower back, aching to pull her to him. How did he become so... blessed? It was the only fitting word to describe what Amanda was to him. A blessing. He wanted this dance to last the entire night, but already the song was ending. "May I ask you do me a small favor?"

"Hmm?"

"Dance one more dance, preferably with a married or older man, and then leave the party."

She brightened as if he'd offered her a gift. "But the party isn't showing any signs of ending, and these things tend to go on until the early hours."

"If you don't leave, one of two problems are going to occur." He forced his shoulders to relax. "The next fop who ogles you is going to wind up with a bloody nose, or I'm going to whirl you into a secluded room and kiss you breathless."

Her lips parted in a silent gasp.

"Either way, we'll have another scandal on our hands."

She blanched, but the music ended, and she hid her expression with a curtsy.

He bowed and escorted her off the floor.

"What of my father?"

"I will speak with him, tomorrow at the club."

Her grip on his arm tightened. "He's in a temper."

"I will win him over." He spoke the words with guileless confidence, more to convince himself than her. He must win back Mr. Klein, or all will be for naught.

CHAPTER 8

*W*esley strode up the steps of the Reading Room gentlemen's club. Van Hassel sat in one of the wicker chairs on the porch, discussing stocks with Mr. James Bennett the second and Commodore Gerry of the New York Yacht Club.

"Ho there, Jansen." Van Hassel held up a copy of the *New York Herald* folded to the business page. "What's your take on the next neat stroke of business?" He pointed to the stocks listing. "What's your pick?"

Wesley stared at the newspaper. Several stock names had been circled, but the letters danced on the page. He tensed, unable to make anything out. His father had died believing Wesley an idiot who couldn't read. It wasn't for a lack of trying on both their parts. Father paid for the best tutors to teach him, and Wesley had stayed up night after night trying to keep the letters in place, to no avail. Wesley had his tricks, though. Van Hassel, Bennett, and the Commodore all stared at him, waiting patiently. He leaned closer and squinted his eyes to bide more time.

"Which ones did you pick?" Maybe they'd come up with the answer for him.

Bennett shook his head. "No influencing the pick. Just give us your gut."

Where was his older brother to bail him out? Or his secretary, for that matter. Theo had aided Wesley through school by reading him his assignments. Once Wesley had graduated—just barely—he'd found the working world easier. He paid a secretary to read things to him as if doing so was beneath him.

Wait. Was that an *N* for Northern? "Ah, Northern Pacific is always a good bet."

Van Hassel shook the page. "Of the circled ones, clever chap."

Wesley ground his teeth at Van Hassel's sarcastic tone. The man's obsession with stock picks grew tiresome. Wesley stared at the newspaper's typeset letters. Was that a *B* or a *D*?

He'd once overheard Theo tell his father that he did Wesley's assignments because he didn't want to be embarrassed by his brother. From that moment forward, Wesley had vowed he'd never let anyone know he was an imbecile.

"That one." He pointed to the circle at the top left.

Van Hassel flipped the newspaper around and drew his chin back, reading the choice. "Truly?"

"That's a bold move, Jansen." Bennett rubbed his beard. "I was considering shorting that stock."

Van Hassel's eyebrows lifted. "You also bet against stocks?"

"Rarely. It's a risky endeavor." Bennett snorted as if he'd lost money and learned a lesson.

Van Hassel stared at the knot in Wesley's cravat as if seeing through him.

"I wouldn't go betting the farm. I'm a bit preoccupied." Wesley craned his neck and peeked inside the club. "Has anyone seen Mr. Klein?"

All three grimaced.

"I do believe he's in the billiard room." The commodore jabbed his thumb toward the club entrance and tipped his hat. "Best of luck to you."

"Thank you, sir." Wesley strode past the shelves of books and men leisurely smoking cigars. He stopped on the threshold of the billiard room and cleared his throat.

Mr. Klein rubbed chalk on the head of his cue and spied Wesley. "Oh, hang it." He flung the chalk down. "I was hoping to relax."

Wesley stepped into the rich mahogany-paneled room with its gold-leafed, coffered ceiling. "Might I have a word with you privately, sir?"

"If I had my druthers, your club membership would

be revoked." Mr. Klein pointed the pool stick at him. "Have you tossed out on your ear."

Wesley pulled the French glass doors shut behind him. "There is business between us that needs addressing." He glanced at the club chairs near the fireplace, but Mr. Klein widened his stance and crossed his arms where he stood.

"Let's get this over with quickly."

"Understood." Wesley cleared his throat. *God, give me the words.* He inhaled a steading breath. "You're a principled man. It's what brought you this far. You inherited your father's company, and with vision and innovation, doubled it."

"In half the time it took him to build it."

"You took bold risks."

"Daily. I put my reputation on the line. It meant putting in the work, too, long hours, connecting with society walkers, and making sacrifices."

"But now you can be measured and weigh your options."

Mr. Klein issued Wesley a stiff nod. "Get to your point."

Wesley hooked his thumbs into his pockets. "You decided to align with Jansen and Sons because our new grade of gasoline will bring our companies to the next level. If I made an alliance with Duryea Motor Wagon Co. instead…"

Mr. Klein's jaw tightened, and his face reddened.

The man didn't seem to like being backed into the corner. Time to give him some leverage.

"My feelings for your daughter haven't changed. I love her and promise to cherish her all the days of my life. I understand what is being said about me, but it's not true." He paused and held Mr. Klein's gaze. "I found Miss Blunt unconscious with Jansen and Sons financial statements on her person. I asked around, and she's the daughter of union boss George Blunt."

"Those unions are mobsters—extortionists." Mr. Klein pounded the end of his cue stick on the floor.

"Foul play is at hand, but not mine. Why would I concede so much to you"—Wesley removed his copy of the signed marriage contract from his trouser pocket— "and then go and blow the whole thing to hades in a matter of hours?" He unfolded the paper and pointed at his signature. "Your copy was delivered to your home address just after midnight that night."

"It's not a stretch of the imagination to believe a young blood would celebrate an agreement, get corned on martinis, and take some floozy back to his apartment."

"Except I don't drink hard liquor, nor am I a bounder. When have you ever seen me with fast women or having more than one glass of wine or champagne?"

Mr. Klein stared at the billiard table between them. "Can't say I have." He rubbed his chin.

"That night, I returned to my office to review the agreement and fell asleep at my desk. I woke to a woman's scream." Wesley widened his stance, matching Mr. Klein's. "I would never do anything to hurt Amanda."

"Then you'll need to prove you're not some Casanova—"

"But—"

"Not just to me, but all of society." Mr. Klein removed the rack from its hook and tossed it on the table. "And Amanda, of course."

Wesley raised his right hand. "God help me, I'll find a way."

Mr. Klein reached into the billiard table pocket and pulled out the polished billiard balls. "Amanda looks like her mother." His thick fingers organized the solids and stripes in the triangular rack. "I loved her, you know—Amanda's mother. She broke my heart and drowned it in the Atlantic. It hurt so much to have that daily reminder in the face of your own daughter. It was one of the reasons I sent her away." He snorted. "I should warn you. Love makes a man weak."

"Vulnerable, yes, but love can also make a person stronger."

Mr. Klein shrugged.

"You created an empire and raised a wonderful daughter."

"She looks like her mother, but her character is more principled. I paid for the best governess and schooling to see to it. I wasn't a good father, but it doesn't mean I didn't love her."

"You did what you could." This was a side of Mr. Klein Wesley hadn't seen.

He jabbed his finger at Wesley. "You need to do better, hear me? Amanda's a quiet girl and observative, but she's taken with you and sparks to life when you're around." He picked up his cue stick and pointed it at Wesley. "I want this deal to go through." He removed the triangle from the racked balls. "So get this nasty rumor cleared up."

"I still have your blessing?"

"Persistent bugger." He sighed. "Prove yourself. This isn't just a business deal. I see a lot of myself in you. If you want my continued blessing, then you need to turn all this talk around as you did last evening. I want my daughter's reputation to be unscathed when she walks down that aisle." He pointed a finger at Wesley's chest and arched an eyebrow. "And yours also."

Wesley swallowed at the tougher proposition but nodded.

Mr. Klein raised his voice. "And if I catch you even sneezing in the direction of another woman, I will not only ride you out of Newport on a rail, but New York, and the entire continental U.S." He raised an eyebrow and shook the cue stick at him. "Got it?"

"Yes, sir."

He gestured to the door. "Now let me work on my game."

Wesley opened the French doors and exited with a

triumphant grin, bumping into Van Hassel just outside the billiard room.

Van Hassel stepped aside. "Pardon, old chap."

Wesley patted him on the shoulder and exited the club with a spritely step. He had a beach date to attend. Wait until Amanda heard the news.

CHAPTER 9

$\mathcal{A}$manda rode to Bailey's beach with Olivia and their lady's maids. The afternoon sun shone bright off the water as she and Olivia exited the bathing houses and picked a spot in the sand near the pavilion. Katie and Olivia's maid spread an oversized blanket and some pillows for them to recline upon.

Ocean breezes wafted cigar smoke from a group of masculine solidarity under the pavilion's arches. The men's occasional bursts of laughter split the air. Was Wesley among them?

Amanda fiddled with the sailor's collar on her bathing costume.

A passing watchman nodded to Olivia. "Good day, Mrs. Van Hassel. Who might this be?" He paused and eyed Amanda as if questioning her Sprouting Rock membership to Bailey's beach.

"This is Miss Amanda Klein. She hasn't summered

in Newport in quite some time. You remember her father, William Klein from Breakwater Court?"

"Indeed." He tipped his hat and moved on. "Enjoy the beautiful day."

Several men exited the pavilion with a ball and circled into two groups. Wesley was indeed among them. His gaze swept the beach, but the only indication he'd spotted her was a flash of a crooked smile. Even still, Amanda's cheeks heated as if sunburned, and she adjusted the brim of her hat.

"I still can't believe Mr. Jansen had the nerve to follow you to Newport after what he did to that woman." Olivia lowered onto the blanket, careful not to upset the horizontal ruffles of her daring white wool serge bathing suit. "He's a perfect vulture to prey upon Miss Blunt, then traipse about Newport while she lies in a hospital bed, perhaps dying from her injuries."

"We don't know the full story." A twinge niggled Amanda's heart. Surely, Wesley wouldn't have left New York before confirming the woman was fine?

"And to show up at the same party as you last night. What a disaster that could have been." Olivia crossed her stockinged ankles. "It was bad enough you received a doctored invitation. Who would have known you planned to attend the Hagen party?"

Wesley's words rang in her mind. *Come to the Hagen party, but don't dance with me right away.*

"He certainly didn't waste time claiming you for a dance. That blooming bounder thinks he can have his tea with a scone on the side. You should have snubbed him. He's hoping if you accept him, the scandal will die down, but getting away with it once will only make him a likely candidate to try again."

Had Wesley danced with her to get people to hold their tongues? "Why would he have tampered with the invitation, then?"

"Don't be a simpleton." Olivia bumped Amanda's shoulder with her own. "To put people's focus on you and not his actions, of course."

The look of surprise on Wesley's face at the Hagen party didn't make Olivia's claim seem likely, but had it all been an act? Had he feigned his declaration of love in the yard? It initially seemed as though he'd come to her rescue at the party, but had she mistaken his intentions?

I promise to prove myself, Wesley had said.

Would he have staged all that to make himself appear the hero, so she'd take him back?

A few men shouted and footsteps thudded in the sand. Wesley jumped and caught the ball midair before another fellow tackled him, sending sand flying in all directions. Wesley pushed to his feet, passed the ball to another player, and assisted the man who'd knocked him down.

Amanda dusted sand off her beach blanket.

You know me. You know my character. Tell me you believe me. She hadn't imagined the vulnerability in Wesley's expression that afternoon on the lawn.

"Miss Klein." Mrs. Tessie Oelrich stopped with her circle of friends. "What a splash you made last evening." Mrs. Oelrich's corset must have been drawn too tight, for she paused periodically to catch her breath. "I daresay, red is going to be the color of the summer."

The other ladies nodded their heads, looking like choreographed singers from the Metropolitan Opera House.

A petite woman with wide puffed sleeves on her bathing costume addressed Amanda. "We're hosting a gathering tomorrow night. An invite has been extended to your family. I do hope you'll come." She glanced at Olivia and added as if an afterthought, "You, too, Olivia."

Amanda had planned to curl up with a book in front of the fire, but Olivia spoke for her. "Of course, we'll be there. We wouldn't miss it." Olivia asked the ladies' opinions of her daring bathing costume, and they launched into a discussion on the latest fashions, but Amanda's mind drifted back to Wesley.

"Your musing fits make you such a bore, Amanda." Olivia rose from the pillows. "Tessie, let's go take in the cure. Hopefully, the water's not too cold." The group of ladies turned to stroll toward the ocean, but Olivia hesitated and looked down on Amanda. "Aren't you going to join us?"

Amanda tilted her head up, and Lily's voice tapped Amanda's conscious. *Bloom where you are planted because God has tilled the soil.* Should she go and better her social situation by trying to make more acquaintances? But what did she have in common with these women—wealthy fathers and a summer cottage along Bellevue Avenue? Her heart thumped an irregular rhythm, and the sand held her feet in place. "Thank you, but no. I'm going to sit here and enjoy the sun's warmth."

"Of course not, you can't be bothered with social drudgery." Olivia released an exasperated sigh and waved to Tessie. "Wait up."

Tessie pivoted, popping her hip out to one side. "Isn't Amanda coming?"

"I don't give a straw what she does." Olivia linked arms with Tessie and strolled toward the water.

Amanda tried not to allow Olivia's barbs to prick her sensitivities, but her accusations held some truth. How long would she allow her fears to limit her?

A cheer rang out over the crash of the waves, and Wesley held up the ball as he crossed the goal line. If only she could hold an eighth of Wesley's natural confidence. The game distracted her for a bit, and she admired Wesley's athleticism until the dizzying black horizontal stripes on the men's swimsuits caused her to look away. How were the players able to tell who was on their team?

Two young women she'd seen at the party but hadn't made their acquaintance strolled along the beach under colorful parasols. They eyed her up and down before waving, and Amanda flashed them a mild smile back.

An odd sensation as if she were being watched lifted the fine hair on the back of Amanda's neck. From the pavilion, Jeffrey Van Hassel and newspaper owner and once-infamous knave, James Gordon Bennett, peered at her.

Jeffrey's gaze slid past her to his wife, Olivia, standing ankle deep in the ocean. He lifted two fingers, and a waiter rushed to his side.

Amanda removed a book from her bag and cracked open the binding to where she'd left off in *The Tale of Two Cities*. Blocking the sounds of beachgoers and waiters rushing to do the members' bidding, she lost herself in the writings of Charles Dickens.

"Pardon me, miss." Katie cleared her throat.

Amanda squinted at her maid silhouetted by the sun.

"A waiter handed me this"—she thrust a folded note in Amanda's direction—"and said it was most urgent."

Amanda unfolded the note.

I must speak with you, privately. Meet me in your bath-house. –Wesley.

Wesley usually signed with just a *W*, but then again, he often dictated his notes for others to write. She glanced down the beach. The rugby game had ended, and the men congregated near the bar under the pavilion arches. Wesley stood on the edge of the crowd but didn't look her way.

A screech riveted her attention toward the ocean as Olivia and the girls held their bathing skirts higher and jumped a whitecapped wave.

Amanda stared at the note. *Privately?* Despite the sun's warm rays, a chill ran through her at the implications of such a risky endeavor. Rumors would fly full chisel if the two of them were caught alone together. But what if he'd heard information exonerating him from Miss Blunt's push down the stairs? Maybe he was second guessing his suggestion for tonight's party, or wanted to review the plan?

"Katie." Amanda folded the note and tucked it into the bodice of her bathing costume. "I want you to join me, but I need to trust you with a secret."

The maid hesitated. "What kind of a secret?" Her pause signified she held confidences with utmost sincerity.

"I'm not certain yet." Amanda rose and dusted sand off her bathing skirt. "Leave our things. This should only take a moment." At least, she hoped. The faster they were in and out of the bathhouse, the better.

Amanda climbed the few wooden stairs to the Klein's beach-side entrance on the row of members' bathhouses and lifted the latch. She entered the Klein's private changing room, and Katie followed, shutting the door behind.

"Halloo?" Amanda whispered into the darkness as

her eyes adjusted to the dim light spilling through the cracks in the wooden siding and from around the street-side door.

The front street entrance of the single-roomed bath-house jerked open, and a large, dark form slipped inside, quickly closing the door.

Amanda gasped.

Katie's hand flew to her bosom, and she stepped back against the clapboard walls.

In one smooth stride, Wesley stood in front of Amanda and gripped her forearms. "What's wrong? Is something a matter?"

"No...I..." Why was he asking her? He'd called this meeting. Shouldn't she be posing those questions to him?

His eyes searched hers under a furrowed brow, and the scent of sun, salt, and sweat enveloped her. "I got your note."

"My note?" His nearness scattered her wits. Hadn't *he* sent her the note?

"I came as soon as I could."

A click sounded outside the oceanfront door.

What was that? Did someone just lock...

Amanda spun and tried the latch.

Locked.

She jiggled it harder, but nothing budged.

"Don't fret. The front is open." Wesley strode to the street entrance, but the knob didn't twist. It, too, was locked. "Dash it. What is this rubbish?" He lowered his shoulder and rammed the door. It merely bounced in the frame. He raised a fisted hand to pound on the wooden panel.

"No!" Amanda lunged, gripping the firm muscles of his upper arm with both hands. "Don't draw attention."

He lowered his arm, and her hands fell to her sides.

A vertical line creased between his eyebrows. "Do you have the key on you?"

She shook her head so rapidly her bathing hat fell askew. "I left it in the bag on the beach."

He raked a hand through his dark waves of hair. "Some schmuck is playing a poor idea of a joke."

A prank that could ruin her. An empty pit opened inside Amanda's stomach.

Katie stepped out of the shadow to right Amanda's hat and adjusted the hair pins to hold it. Thank goodness for her presence.

"Treachery again," Wesley muttered. He paced the small area and peered up at the rafters with a grim expression. "Your father will withdraw his blessing and run me out of the country over being discovered in your changing room, even if your maid was present."

Her father would be enraged. Rumors would deem her a harlot like her mother. He'd send her packing or marry her to some overseas noble to never have to look upon her face again.

"There must be a way out." He bounced on the floorboards as if to render one loose.

Katie folded her hands and bent her head as if praying.

Amanda, too, sent up a prayer. *Lord, please prevent a scandal.*

Wesley squatted and tried to pry up a board with his fingers but gave up after a quick attempt. Was he behind this? Both Jansen and Sons and Klein & Co. profited from their union. Had he written the note to try to force her to the marriage altar as Olivia had suggested? Bile rose in Amanda's throat.

"Don't fret." Wesley tilted her chin up with his index finger. "We're going to figure a way out." His amber eyes held hers.

"You've been set up." Katie leaned the back of her head against the wall, her gaze sliding between Wesley and Amanda. "Someone wanted to trap you in here." She looked to Wesley. "Who gave you the note?"

He frowned. "A waiter, I believe."

"A shorter man, slender build, with the makings of a mustache and beard." She held her hand flat a couple inches above her head. "About this tall."

"That's right." The line between his furrowed eyebrows deepened.

"The same waiter handed us a letter too." Amanda removed the note tucked in her bodice and passed it to Wesley.

He barely glanced at the writing before flinging the paper to the floor. "Hang it." Wesley resumed his pacing at an increased tempo. "First, the woman falling down the stairs, the red dress invitation, and now this. Someone is purposefully trying to ruin us."

Amanda shook her head. "I don't understand. Why would someone stage the accident on the stairs to break off our engagement, but then lock us in a bath house together so we'd be forced to marry to save my reputation?"

Wesley squeezed his eyes closed. "I met with your father this morning." He opened his eyes and sighed. "All in all, the meeting went rather well. We continue to have his blessing, but he threatened loud enough for the men in the club to hear that if your reputation isn't left unscathed, he'd ride me out of town on a rail."

Someone didn't want their engagement to go through, but who? And why?

The horn of a motor car honked from the street side.

A low whistle followed, and a distant voice said, "That's a beaut, old chap."

Katie gasped. "Danny." She pressed her hands to her cheeks. "Miss, I may know a way out..." She swallowed as if the thought pained her.

"What is it?" Amanda inched closer to her maid.

"Please don't get me or Danny fired." Katie crinkled the apron of her uniform. "We need our jobs because we plan on getting married and starting a family."

Most employers frowned upon servants dating, but to avoid scandal, Amanda would take this secret to the grave. "I won't tell a soul. I promise."

Katie glanced at Wesley, who nodded his consent. She strode to the door and whistled a bird call. Katie peered at Amanda. "It's how we arrange to meet—just to talk, is all."

The three of them waited in silence. Katie whistled again.

"Katie-girl?" Danny whispered on the other side of the door. "Are you alone?"

Katie leaned against the door and spoke toward the seam. "We're trapped. Can you pick the lock and not be noticed?"

"Gee whiz, Katie." His footsteps walked away and then back. "You're gonna get us in the soup. Please tell me you didn't say that in front of your employer."

"She promised she won't tell." Katie glanced back at Amanda, and she nodded. "It's a matter of utmost importance."

Danny fell silent once more.

A knock sounded on the oceanside door. "Amanda, are you in there?"

Amanda jumped, recognizing the voice, and gripped the front of Wesley's bathing costume. "It's Olivia," she murmured. "What do I say?"

Wesley curved an arm around her shoulder, drawing her close, and whispered in her ear.

"I'm here." Amanda cleared her throat and called out to Olivia, "I thought I left something."

"Don't be a four-flusher with me," Olivia said in a stern tone.

She covered her mouth to hide her gasp. Olivia didn't believe her. Was Olivia saying she knew Amanda was in here with Wesley?

"I know you too well. You're hiding from people, and we both know it." Olivia rattled the latch. "We're about to start a card game at the pavilion, and we need a fourth player."

Wesley brushed aside a tendril of Amanda's hair, swirling heat through her stomach and chest, and whispered instructions. His breath tickled her ear and sent shivers along her skin.

"Just a minute." She cleared the rasp from her voice. "I dropped the key and have to find it."

Danny's voice murmured across the room. "Quick. Slide two of your hairpins under the door."

Katie stuck her hand under her cap and did as asked.

Mumbling could be heard from behind the front door about getting booted from their jobs and him being a lunkhead.

Wesley's arm remained around Amanda like a protective shield. It was inappropriate for him to be so near, and she should step away, but instead, she leaned into his strength and courage.

"Amanda?" Olivia knocked on the back door. "What's taking so long?"

Wesley's warm palm slid from her arm to her upper back, and his thumb stroked her spine. The intimate touch felt as natural as how Lily's parents interacted with each other. His amber eyes, steady with candid confidence, reassured her. He dipped his chin, encouraging her to speak.

She swallowed. "You might have to go on without me."

A quiet moment passed with only the sound of Wesley's rhythmic breathing and a clinking of metal in the front lock.

"I'll wait." Olivia heaved a sigh.

It wasn't like her friend to be patient. Could she have written the notes? Olivia had been the one to inform Amanda of Cynthia Blunt's fall. She'd also been at Breakpoint Manor when the invitation to the Hagen party arrived. Olivia could be superficial, but she'd helped Amanda survive boarding school. She wouldn't do something so malicious. Would she?

"Got it," Danny's voice whispered.

"I'll sneak out with Danny." Wesley pressed a kiss to Amanda's temple. "Wait a few minutes, then exit the front and slide around the back to meet Olivia."

The knob turned and the door cracked open. In a flash, Wesley disappeared and Danny with him. Only the residual warmth of Wesley's touch remained.

～

*W*esley crept along the front of the bathhouses with Danny falling in step beside him. The smart lad had pulled the Klein carriage close to block the view of others. "How'd you learn to pick a lock?"

Danny's gaze darted everywhere but wouldn't meet Wesley's. "I had a not-so-good upbringing in Ireland, but Katie's helped me mend my ways. She's got me going to church and praying, but I'll always be a tinkerer."

Wesley drew up short and fumbled in his bathing costume pocket for a key. He checked the number with the number of his brother's bathhouse and opened the door. "Wait here a moment."

Danny stood erect with his chin high and hands folded in front of him like a sentinel. Wesley clapped him on the arm before stepping inside and donning his clothes. He exited minutes later in light-tan trousers, a cream shirt, waistcoat, and tie with a blue-striped jacket.

"Walk with me a bit. I have a proposition for you, and Tiverton Bluff is only few blocks away." Wesley meandered to the road.

Danny traversed beside him but kept looking back at the Klein carriage.

"Their card game will last an hour or two. Plenty of time to get back." Wesley turned down the street toward Crossways, the unique Colonial Revival-style home owned by Mamie and Stuyvesant Fish, renowned for their outlandish parties. "Tell me about your plans, Mr...."

"Daniel Kelly, sir. At your service."

One side of Wesley's mouth lifted. He liked the lad's enthusiasm.

"I've always taken things apart and enjoyed puttin' them back together. I like to know how things work. Me mum hated to come home and find pieces of her grandfather clock labeled and lyin' on a sheet across the floor."

"How did you become a driver?"

"Pop worked as one and had me drivin' a carriage ever since my feet could reach the floorboards."

Wesley turned right onto Ruggles Avenue. A stretch of tall green hedges blocked the manor homes from view. A motor car rumbled around a turn.

"That's where the future lies." A smile spread across Danny's face. The driver honked and waved as he passed but wasn't recognizable underneath the dust hood and goggles. Danny pivoted to watch the motor car zip down Bellevue Ave.

"I agree." Wesley stuffed his hands into his pockets. "Ever tinker with an engine?"

"I wish I could say I have."

"Your next day off, I want you to pay a visit to a friend of mine who runs a motorcar engine research and development team. He summers just south of here. I'll pen him a note to expect you."

"That's capital." Danny added a little jump to his step. He stopped and pumped Wesley's hand. "Thank you, Mr. Jensen."

"My pleasure." Wesley's smile widened. "I'm going

to have my accountant transfer a share of stock into your name for taking a risk today. Jansen and Sons stock dipped recently, but I have big plans for the company."

Danny blinked. "I don't know what to say. Thank you."

"Think of it as an early wedding present."

The lad's face reddened, and a shy smile bloomed on his lips.

"Go on back and keep a protective eye on our ladies. Let me know if anyone tries to pull another prank."

"Yes, sir." Danny stood at attention. He issued him a salute and darted back toward Ocean Drive.

Wesley smiled and shook his head as he resumed his walk, turning down the lane to Tiverton Bluff. Unlike reading and writing, connecting people came naturally to him. His father's objective had been to make as much money as humanly possible, and Wesley's brother had followed suit but enjoyed spending as well as earning. Wesley felt called to a greater purpose. He wanted to grow the company, to better people's lives, for those who purchased their engine fuel and those employed by Jansen and Sons.

He nodded to the gardener planting rows of red flowers.

The butler swung the door open and took Wesley's straw skimmer hat as he entered. The vanilla-cherry scent of a smoked cigar hung in the air.

"Master Theodore has arrived, sir, and requested for you to meet him in his study upon your return."

Theo was here, already? Was that a good sign regarding Miss Blunt's recovery? He followed the cherry-smoke smell across the Italian marbled floors in the direction of the study.

Theo stood facing a window framed with heavy tasseled draperies with a drink in his hand.

"I didn't expect you here so soon," Wesley greeted his brother. "But it's great to see you." He clapped Theo on the back. "What is the word on Miss Blunt? How is she faring?"

Theo stiffened. "She, ah"—he cleared his throat— "suffered a broken leg but is recovering at home." His gaze flicked to the corner of the room.

Wesley pivoted.

"You remember Detective Millis." Theo pointed his glass at the man seated in the low-backed chair near the grate.

How could he forget the detective who'd appeared while the doctor aided Miss Blunt?

A derisive smile curved Detective Millis's lips. He raised his highball glass and tipped his head at Wesley. "Have you handled your pressing business in Newport?"

Was this an ambush? "I'm still working to repair the damage this bizarre situation has caused." Wesley hooked his thumbs into his pockets. "Have you uncovered the reason why Miss Blunt was in the Jansen and Sons' office building after hours?"

"Turns out Miss Blunt is the daughter of one of the higher ups in the American Federation of Labor."

Wesley nodded. "So you've confirmed her father sent her to obtain classified company information. That explains why my desk drawer was open and the papers in her purse."

"Or did you plant the papers to look less guilty?" Detective Millis tossed back the rest of his drink. "Miss Blunt claims she was invited by you, after topping off a couple bottles of champagne."

"That's a lie." Heat filled Wesley's chest, inching up his throat, and he swallowed to keep it down. Had Miss Blunt seen the half glass of champagne on his desk and added that to her story to con the detective? "What time did she say she arrived? Where was she before the incident?"

"Miss Blunt"—the detective rose—"has become tight-lipped after a visit from your brother."

Wesley eyed Theo, who tried to hold his gaze but failed. What had Theo done?

"I must be going." Detective Millis set his glass on the table. "But I plan to hang around with you Newport la-di-da types for a while. I'll be staying at the Ocean House Hotel, if any new information comes to light or to your memory." He nodded to Theo. "I appreciate you getting me added to the Gibbons' guest list. I will see you tonight."

Wesley waited in silence until the butler closed the door behind the detective, before rounding on his brother. "What is going on?"

Theo waved his hand in a dismissive manner. "Don't take his guff. He's new to the job and overly eager to make a name for himself. If need be, I'll go over his head."

"And do what?"

"Plunk down a couple hundred to make him drop the case." Theo snorted.

Miss Blunt has become tight-lipped after a visit from your brother. "Did you pay Miss Blunt to remain silent?"

"It was for the best." Theo slumped into a chair with a shrug. "Why are you being so sensitive?"

"Because it makes me appear guilty." Wesley pressed his palms to his temples. Mr. Klein's voice raged in his head. *I want your reputation unscathed when you walk down that aisle.*

"It's not the first time I paid to get you out of a fix."

"What do you mean?" Wesley narrowed his gaze.

"How do you think you graduated? I had to grease some palms for that feat."

A jolt ran through Wesley. "I never asked you to do that."

"You didn't have to. Brothers take care of one another." He sipped from his glass. "Relax. You need a drink."

Wesley shook his head. "What I need is the truth. What did Miss Blunt say when you visited her?"

A muscle in Theo's jaw twitched. "Are you going to pester me like the detective?"

"I need to clear my name."

"It's all going to blow over. Just give it time."

"I don't want this stain on my reputation. Amanda's father won't condone our marriage, and even if he did, I don't want Amanda questioning my character. Marriages are built on trust."

Theo's gaze lowered. He tossed back the rest of his drink and rose. "I'm late to meet the boys at the club. I'll see you later at the Gibbons' party."

His brother fled the room, leaving a stockpile of questions unanswered. How many bribes had Theo paid on his behalf? Did he think Wesley couldn't handle himself? How could the upstanding older brother who Wesley admired resort to bribing people?

CHAPTER 10

$\mathcal{A}$manda regretted allowing Olivia to accept tonight's invitation for her. Their host, Mrs. Grace Gibbons—who wore a red gown, as did several other ladies—organized the guests into groups for charades. Why couldn't they have gone to a play or a musical where Amanda could have sat and listened without needing to interact?

Wesley entered late with his brother and a stern-faced fellow Amanda hadn't seen before.

Olivia raised her fan and whispered in Amanda's ear. "Who is the dingy fellow beside Mr. Jansen?"

Amanda shrugged one shoulder.

"The Jansens really shouldn't associate with the like." Olivia snorted. "They're under enough suspicion already. I'm surprised someone so shabby would have the gall to show their face at a party like this. He's not worthy to shine our shoes."

Amanda lost her patience with Olivia's high-and-mighty opinions. "Wasn't Jesus born in a manger to poor parents? Would you not welcome the King of Kings if He arrived at the door?"

Olivia sipped her champagne glass. "We'd make an exception because of His bloodline."

Amanda couldn't stop the flow of words now that she'd begun. "Last I remember, Jesus came for all mankind, not just elites."

"Good for you"—A smile grew across Olivia's face—"becoming all high and mighty. You may hold the courage to run with our set after all."

"Welcome, Mr. Jansen." Grace practically yanked Amanda from her chair to partner her with Wesley. "How about you pair with Miss Klein, and Mr. and Mrs. Van Hassel can be a group?"

A jaunty smile raised one side of Wesley's mouth, and he lowered his voice so only Amanda could hear. "I think our hostess is hoping for her party to be all the talk tomorrow."

Amanda groaned.

Theo was matched with Mr. Zackary Faulkner, owner of Faulkner Gaslight Company, his wife, and his lovely daughter of a marriageable age. Mr. Faulkner was Jansen and Sons' biggest client.

"Your brother's speaking with Faulkner." Jeffrey motioned his glass in their direction. "Has Faulkner's business shown any signs of growth lately?"

"Relax, Van Hassel." Wesley tapped the back of his

hand on Jeffrey's arm and said in a teasing tone, "You can work on getting stock tips later."

Jeffrey reddened and tugged on his collar.

Mrs. Gibbons attempted to add the stranger to the group, but he declined to participate. Instead, he wandered over and sat near the wall, but Amanda could feel his eyes on her.

"Who's the man who arrived with you?" Amanda asked Wesley quietly, but both Olivia and Jeffrey leaned closer to hear the answer.

Wesley's smile fell. "He's a detective from New York."

Amanda held in her gasp. Was Wesley being investigated? She didn't want to ask any further questions as Olivia listened with her gossiping tongue.

"Here are your phrases to act out as a group." Mrs. Gibbons handed a paper to Wesley.

He nodded and held it out for them to read.

Jeffrey knocked his hand down. "Don't show it to the entire room. Read it and whisper it to us."

Wesley paled. He gripped the paper with both hands and stared at it. "It's...uh." He shuffled his feet. "Give me a moment. My eyes need to adjust."

"Don't tell us you need glasses, because I've played lawn tennis against you." Jeffrey motioned with a pretend racket. "I've never seen someone track a ball like Jansen."

"Indeed." Wesley's Adam's apple bobbed, and he peered at the paper again.

The other groups murmured, working out their skits and getting a significant head start.

Amanda peeked over his shoulder at the phrase and whispered to the group, "'Drive a motor car to the beach.'"

Wesley's shoulders relaxed, and he wiped his forehead with the back of his hand. "I've got it." He waved them close and explained the parts they were to play. Amanda and Olivia pretended to hold up their skirts as they jumped the waves, and Wesley and Jeffrey honked and pulled up alongside. Wesley went as far as to lift his pretend goggles when he spied the women.

When their turn came, the other guests guessed their scenario right away. The detective remained in his corner, assessing Wesley with a grim expression. The other groups performed, but the detective's unswerving gaze remained on their group. As their team's turn rolled around again, Wesley gestured for Amanda to read the paper.

"'Stock market slump.'" She peered at Wesley. "How do we enact stocks dropping?"

Wesley suggested they pretend to be stock traders on the exchange floor signaling to buy and then switching to sell.

As her husband rose, Olivia placed her hand on his sleeve. "Jeffrey, where are you going?"

"Enough of this game. I need another drink." He disappeared into the next room while the rest of the groups acted out their charades.

A deep sadness shadowed Olivia's eyes. Was their marriage strained? Did Jeffrey overly imbibe? Olivia spied Consuela Vanderbilt and raised her hand, scurrying away to catch her attention. When their turn for charades came, Amanda apologized and told their hostess they'd sit this round out.

Amanda glanced again at the detective. What information did he think to obtain at a party? Shouldn't he be in New York questioning Miss Blunt? Was he here to discover the truth or just confirm his suspicions that Wesley had something to do with Miss Blunt's accident?

The detective's gaze finally slid from Wesley to follow Jeffrey as he signaled a servant for a drink and stopped to speak to their hostess.

Wesley gripped her hand and pressed the back of it to his lips. His warm gaze held hers. "Don't fret over the detective. God willing, the truth finds a way to surface."

Amanda swallowed. "Then I'll be praying God's will be done quickly."

Charades ended, and Mrs. Gibbons announced a break for food and refreshments, to be followed by a special reading.

"We haven't yet been introduced." The detective appeared at her elbow.

Wesley stiffened. "Miss Klein, this is—"

"Detective Millis from the upper west side." He bowed formally. "A pleasure to meet you, although I question your company." He quirked a grin as if he and Wesley were longtime college chums. "I can understand why Mr. Jansen fled New York to follow you to Newport, for you are quite lovely."

A poem Lily often quoted stole past Amanda's lips, "'Praise brings envy...'"

"'And wealth blinds over all. Savor no more, than 'tis good that you recall.'" Detective Millis dipped his chin in salute. "Geoffrey Chaucer—and may truth deliver us, indeed." He turned to Wesley. "Quick witted and a pretty face. No wonder you willingly surrendered a fourth of your assets to her father as a marriage stipulation."

Amanda gasped, and Wesley confirmed the accusation by firing a glare at the detective.

"My father sold me?" Amanda's hands and feet turned numb.

"It wasn't like that." Wesley tried to hold her hand, but she snatched it away. "I asked for his blessing, and your father pressed me to prove the extent of my love. We agreed on a union of the two companies. I would have signed over even more except I need to provide for you in the lifestyle you deserve until our new engine fuel takes off."

Amanda staggered back a step. Detective Millis gripped her elbow to steady her, and she stared at his hand as if it were a poisonous snake.

"Don't touch her, you cad." Wesley fisted his hands, prepared to fight.

Detective Millis released her and stepped back, holding up his palms.

Amanda escaped out the nearest exit into the servant's back hall, hoping no one would see the tears forming.

Wesley followed and stopped her.

"You know that I'm not what everyone has made me out to be." She shook her head. "I'm not the latest thing or some prestigious elite to emulate. These people terrify me, and they misconstrue my fear as condescension. I can't let you overpay for a farce. As it is, I will hinder your business relationships. For I won't be able to host any balls or dinner parties."

"You don't give yourself enough credit, and those things mean little to me." Wesley clasped her gloved hand between his own. "It's the timid woman who finds all this pomp and circumstance ridiculous, who laughs at my sarcastic remarks, and who revels in the beauty of a single flower—she has captured my heart. I love you, and I would agree to all that and more to spend the rest of my days with you by my side."

"But what if people find out that you paid my father to wed me?"

A servant squeezed past them with a tray of finger food.

The detective, who must have followed them into the hall, plucked a cracker with paté off the tray as the waiter passed.

Wesley rounded on him. "Could you not extend us the courtesy of a private moment?"

Detective Millis popped the cracker into his mouth, chewed, and swallowed.

Amanda schooled her features.

Finally, the detective raised his hand in a dismissive wave. "I've heard what I needed to hear." He leaned half out the door. "However, it sounds as though Mr. Jansen is being summoned. I'd best return with you for appearances' sake."

"We'll finish this conversation later," Wesley whispered to Amanda and gestured for her to go ahead.

Detective Millis held the door as she re-entered the library.

"There you are." Mrs. Gibbons strode over and linked her arm around Wesley's, escorting him to the front of the room. "May I have everyone's attention?" Her voice rose above the din of the crowd and conversations died. "I have been informed that Mr. Jansen requested to read a special poem from the works of Longfellow." She handed him a book with a gold-lettered title, *The Complete Works of Henry Longfellow*.

Wesley blanched.

The detective grunted beside Amanda and muttered under his breath, "This should be interesting."

She tore her gaze from Wesley, who grew paler by the second, and eyed Detective Millis. What did he mean by that?

Wesley tried to hand the book back to Mrs. Gibbons, but she walked away, taking a seat in the front row. He flipped open the book. Were his hands shaking?

Images flashed in her memory of cards she'd received from him with the signature only a handwritten *W*, him discarding the note she'd showed him in the bathhouse unread, him wanting to tell her all the things he felt instead of writing them in a letter, him passing her the charade paper.

A glisten of sweat shone on Wesley's forehead. He stared at the page and blinked, flipping to another and repeating the process. The entire room watched—his brother, the detective, Jeffrey and Olivia, Mr. Faulkner, and other business associates. A familiar cough sounded just outside the library. Even her father.

Merciful heavens. Could Wesley not read?

He cleared his throat. "There are so many wonderful works by Longfellow, I don't know if I can choose."

How had she not realized? Amanda's stomach dropped as if falling through a trapdoor, and a cold sweat broke over her body. How many times had she had this feeling at a party, trying to make small talk when Wesley swooped in to save her?

"Pardon, I seem to have something in my throat." He coughed into his hand. "I might need some water."

Was this another practical joke? Why would someone embarrass him like this? His career was on the line...and their future together.

Mrs. Gibbons waited on the edge of her seat for him

to begin. Olivia pursed her lips while Jeffrey snorted and crossed his arms. The detective shifted his feet as if uncomfortable, and the rest of the guests in the room squirmed in their seats, growing impatient.

"Get on with it, Jansen. Time's wasting," an elderly guest shouted.

"I... uh..." Wesley stared at the page, sweat running down his temple.

Wasn't anyone going to intervene? *God, please, a lightning strike, anything.*

She had to help him. Wesley glanced up. The alarm in his gaze squeezed her heart. Had it only been two weeks ago when they'd escaped to the balcony, his gaze so sure—so confident—as he recited her a poem?

Amanda's lips parted. *One he'd memorized.*

"It's not Longfellow." Amanda startled at the sound of her own voice. "The poem you seek was written by Lord Bryon."

Wesley eyed her as if she'd taken leave of her senses, probably because she'd never addressed an entire room before.

She strode to the bookshelf and removed *The Complete Works of Lord Byron*, searched the contents, and found the proper poem. She flipped to the proper page. "You said *She Walks in Beauty* was your favorite. Here it is."

He closed the Longfellow book and set it aside.

She held her spine so stiff, if anyone bumped her, she'd shatter. But she raised her chin and addressed the guests. "After this reading, you'll see how Mr. Jansen drew my affections toward him." She handed the volume to Wesley.

Understanding dawned on his face, and he accepted the book Amanda offered him with a wobbly smile. He cleared his throat once again. "Of course."

Amanda backed to the side of the room near the bookshelf and stood with her hands clasped in front of her.

"'She walks in beauty, like the night.'" Wesley's voice wavered in the first line, but by the second stanza, it rose and fell in iambic tetrameter. His undaunted self-assurance returned, and he promenaded around the front of the room with the Gibbons Italian marble fireplace as the backdrop. He worked the crowd and even kneeled, daring to lift the hand of Mrs. Caroline Astor, reciting the stanza about waves of raven tresses. Mrs. Astor cracked a smile and fanned her face with a Chinese folded fan.

He rose along with the volume of his voice and abruptly turned to look at Amanda for the third stanza.

She pressed her back into the wooden shelves. The guests' gazes honed in on her, and scalding heat rose into her cheeks. Her father studied her with a deep vertical crease between his eyebrows. Olivia scowled. Mr. Millis rubbed his chin. The rest of the room sat poised like dogs, salivating for a treat.

Wesley locked eyes with hers and stepped closer. "So calm, so eloquent."

She was taken back in her mind to the balcony cloaked in moonlight, her heart thudding in her chest. Wesley's lips curved up on one side in an appreciative smile, and a sensual flame blazed in his eyes. Her heart devoured his words like a train eating up the track. His gratitude radiated in his warm gaze.

She'd thwarted the plan of whomever attempted to humiliate them for a third time. She no longer felt like a pawn in a chess game where other players determined the rules. Perhaps she didn't need to be intimidated. Maybe she could be the queen, and it was her turn to say, *checkmate*. Wesley's expression sobered, and his voice rippled like a pulse along her skin as he finished with the last line. "'A heart whose love is innocent.'"

He blinked at her for a moment as if startled by his own vehemence.

Her chest heaved, and she could hear her breathless gasps in the stillness of the room.

Wesley stepped back and turned to face the crowd.

The room erupted in cheers and clapping. Ladies fanned their faces, and the men chuckled to relieve the tension.

Mrs. Gibbons stood and thanked Wesley for his passionate delivery. Wesley bowed to Mrs. Gibbons and then to the crowd, but as he straightened, his eyes narrowed.

Amanda followed his gaze out the back of the room to where Wesley's brother peeked both ways before he escorted the daughter of Jansen and Sons' best client outdoors with his hand a little too low on Miss Faulkner's back.

Please Lord, let Theodore Jansen's interest in Miss Faulkner be benign, not only because he could harm business, but also because he was married.

CHAPTER 11

*W*esley excused himself to Mrs. Gibbons, Amanda, and most of the guests who'd converged upon him with congratulations or to discuss Lord Byron's poem. He must speak with Theo before he departed with Miss Faulkner.

"You are too kind." Wesley nodded to Mrs. Elizabeth Lehr paying him a compliment. Her eyes shone with a deep longing for the love he'd described in the poem. He squeezed in between her and Mr. Pembroke Jones, who asked him to recite at one of his wife's parties.

"Let me think on it." Wesley strode to the door.

The butler turned to retrieve Wesley's hat, but Wesley stopped him. "I'm merely getting a bit of air."

He exited the manor in time to see the footman close the carriage on a giggling Miss Faulkner. "Hold up," he yelled to the servant. Wesley marched to the conveyance and rapped on the door's window. "May I?"

He took the lantern from the footman and dismissed him to the bumper seat.

The laughter inside ceased, and his brother mumbled, "Rats, what is it?" Theo opened the door and peered out, leaning across Miss Faulkner to do so.

"Theo." Wesley held open the door with his other hand. "Where are you off to with Miss Faulkner?"

Theo leaned back but shifted in his seat to face Wesley. "Miss Faulkner asked me to escort her to the Casino Club to meet some friends."

Miss Faulkner's gaze lowered to her lap.

"Which friends?" Wesley studied her expression.

She shrugged a dainty shoulder and partially covered her mouth with her gloved fingers. "Consuelo and Grace Vanderbilt"—she hiccupped—"and Tessie Oelrich."

Miss Faulkner was a terrible liar and had sipped a little too much champagne. Wesley peered at Theo. "What would Clarissa think of you gallivanting around with young ladies for a nightcap?"

"I'm merely seeing Miss Faulkner safely to her friends." Theo snorted. "It's not as though you caught us mugging."

Miss Faulkner glanced at Theo, and even in the dim lantern light, the guilty color rising in her cheeks was visible.

Theo crossed his arms. "I don't need to explain myself to you."

"You're married with two precious children and

another on the way." Wesley gestured to Miss Faulkner, who shrank back into the seat cushions. "She's the unmarried daughter of our biggest client. You don't see what could go wrong?"

"Pardon." Miss Faulkner scooted toward the exit, and Wesley aided her out of the carriage. She darted inside the house with her head down.

"Gee whiz!" Theo spit the words like a curse. "Look what you've gone and done."

The hero worship of his older brother shattered, rocking Wesley on his heels. "How long have you been running around behind Clarissa's back?"

His brother merely glared at him. The memory of a woman's crumpled form at the bottom of Jansen and Sons' stairs and the sound of retreating footsteps down a hallway resurfaced.

Wesley narrowed his eyes. "It was you that night at the office." He lowered his voice. "Amanda and I saw you with Miss Blunt earlier that night. You told me you went to the club, but you brought Miss Blunt back to our office afterward, didn't you?"

Theo's mouth opened as if to defend himself, but he said nothing.

"You have the key. When she woke, she mistook me for you. Did you know she went through our files? She's the daughter of a union boss and had last month's income statement sticking out of her purse. You welcomed a wolf into the hen house."

"I was tanked up on Manhattans." He grabbed the

lapel of Wesley's jacket. "She jested about going to the office. We had a few more drinks…"

Theo closed his eyes, but whether it was to try and remember or out of shame, Wesley couldn't tell.

"I passed out, and when I woke, she wasn't on the couch. A lamp was lit in your office, and I caught her exiting. I approached her on the stairs, but I didn't push her. I swear on my life, she tripped on her hem and fell." Theo rubbed his temples. "I tried to help her, but then I heard you, and I panicked."

"Why didn't you say something the next morning?"

Theo's face paled. "Clarissa was there, and she doesn't need to hear about this. It would only complicate matters between us. She's been busy since the kids were born, distant."

"You *need* to be faithful to your wife."

"I covered for you all those years to hide that you can't read. It's your turn to protect me." Theo's words pierced Wesley's heart.

"I never asked you to lie for me." He'd idolized his older brother who was smart, athletic, and a good businessman, while Theo believed his younger brother to be a simpleton. All the business dealings and contracts Wesley had brought into the company meant nothing. To Theo, Wesley had always been inept because he couldn't read. "You did it because you were ashamed of me."

"You think clients would work with us if they knew you'd failed out of school? Don't act so high and mighty.

You haven't been forthright about your well-kept secret. Is Miss Klein even aware?"

After tonight's debacle, she knew now. Yet instead of scoffing, she'd helped him.

"There were consequences because of what you did. A woman was hurt, and you paid her to stay quiet, didn't you? How long are you going to let her blackmail you, until Jansen and Sons is bankrupt?" Wesley stepped back, his stomach bottoming out. "You were going to have me take the fall. I almost lost Amanda over this, and I still might if I can't prove myself to her father. And what about Detective Millis, were you going to let him throw me in jail for something I didn't do?"

"You'll land on your feet." Theo's tone leaked with bitterness. "You always do. Besides, that tiresome chap is a perfect vulture, but he has nothing substantial to go on. He's bluffing."

"Go home, Theo. Enough of your jiggery-pokery." Wesley's jaw clenched. "Go home and confess to your wife before I prove my innocence. She deserves to hear the truth from you."

"You selfish—"

Wesley closed the carriage door and nodded to the driver, who snapped the reins. The vehicle rumbled down the road, and a heaviness fell over him. He'd had to work twice as hard as the other boys to finish school and make his way in life, but now he thanked God for the struggle. If he'd had it easy, he might have ended up like his brother—entitled, rationalizing why it was okay for him to have an affair, paying for secrecy, and indulging in drink. With a heavy heart, Wesley turned back to the Gibbons' party. He took a step and froze.

Detective Millis stood outside the entrance.

Blast. How much had he overheard? Wesley strode toward the front door. "Detective." He nodded and tried to walk past him, but the detective pressed his palm to Wesley's chest. Wesley had no choice but to stop and look the man in the eye.

"There's more to this than your brother is aware. He was set up. Someone paid Miss Blunt to entertain your brother and obtain inside information to take down Jansen and Sons."

Wesley scoffed. "Yeah, her father, the union boss."

Detective Millis shook his head. "He was furious to learn what his daughter had been paid to do. Can't fake that reaction."

"Then who?"

"That's what I'm here to find out." The detective lowered his arm and hooked his thumbs in his pockets. "I've seen enough to know that someone is out to humiliate you and Miss Klein. They don't want a merger to happen, and they're getting desperate." He tipped his hat. "Watch your back. Good night, Mr. Jansen."

Wesley stared after the man strolling down the lane back toward town. Theo being set up still didn't exonerate his infidelity. His heart clenched at how the affair would hurt Clarissa.

As he strode inside, the detective's words, *they're getting desperate,* rang in Wesley's ears. Hadn't whomever this was already gone to great lengths? Wesley swallowed. What else was this person willing to do? He must protect Amanda and save their future.

~

The following morning, his brother's study still reeked of gin, and the entire decanter was missing. Wesley checked on Theo, opening his chamber door a crack. His brother lay sprawled on top of the bed covers, still wearing last night's clothes and snoring like a bear. The empty crystal decanter lay sideways on the Axminister rug, and glass shards littered a corner. On the wall above, a mark suggested the sniffer glass had been thrown and shattered on impact.

Since his brother would be sporting one spanking headache when he awoke, Wesley headed to the Casino Club. The *New York Herald* owner James Gordon Bennett was usually there at this time and his fellow chaps, Charles Longfellow, the writer's son, and Captain Henry Candy, whom Bennett referred to by his nickname, Sugar. He joined them for a game of lawn tennis and drummed up Bennett's interest to write an article about their new gasoline grade. The physical activity cleared his mind, and when they finished, he wiped the sweat from his brow and joined the men for a drink at the bar.

There Van Hassel sat hunched over his glass and perked up as Wesley and the group arrived.

"A lemonade, truly?" Bennett teased Wesley after he ordered. "I didn't take you for a milksop, Jansen."

The other men snickered and ordered a Manhattan, gimlet, and a corpse reviver.

"I like to keep a clear head for an edge above the competition." Wesley nudged Longfellow, reminding the chap he'd been bested twice by the slice on Wesley's serve.

"The sun was in my eyes." Longfellow snorted.

"I was thinking of taking the yacht out this afternoon." Van Hassel sipped his drink and peered at Wesley. "Care to meet us at Goat Island?"

"Capital idea." Bennett clinked his glass to Van Hassel's. "Jansen, plan to sail with me. We can discuss your new engine product further."

"My wife insists on tagging along and bringing Miss Klein." Van Hassel's lips pursed as if he was annoyed, but was it due to the women or because Bennett infringed on his plans?

Wesley straightened. *Amanda.* Detective Millis's warning rang in his head. *They're getting desperate.* Perhaps he should confer with the detective.

Bennett nodded to Captain Candy. "We can recruit a few more ladies and have them host a late luncheon afterward."

"I'll see you later, then." Wesley gulped down his lemonade. He must keep a close eye on Amanda.

CHAPTER 12

*A*manda climbed aboard the *Lucky Turn* and stood next to Olivia. However, the extra-wide mutton sleeves of Olivia's gown filled a foot or two of space, and she had to lean close to yell over the flapping of the luffing sail. "Jeffrey is a capable sailor?"

"Indeed." Olivia sat at the stern and patted a cushion next to her for Amanda.

Amanda gripped the rail as she made her way over. Father had never purchased another yacht after his captain absconded with it and Mother. The ship capsized during a storm off the coast of Georgia, and Amanda hadn't sailed since.

"Permission to come aboard?"

Amanda spun at the sound of Wesley's voice.

Jeffrey glanced up from the helm. "Just make sure you tell Bennett that about *Lucky Turn*'s fin keel and take a look at her rigging."

Wesley whistled. "It's a beauty. Bennett will want to race when he sees this." He stepped into the boat and nodded to Jeffrey and Olivia before turning to Amanda. "Might I have a word?"

She nodded, and he touched her elbow, drawing her aside. The sober expression in place of his usual jaunty smile twisted her nerves into tight coils. He recapped his encounter with Theo and the detective's warning, and she fought not to display emotion. Had Theo Jansen been behind all of this? But he'd only just arrived in Newport for the Gibbons' party.

Her gaze slid to Olivia. She'd been there for the red-dress invitation, the Bailey's Beach bathhouse lock-in, and last night's forced poetry reading. Was she jealous of Amanda's social rise and trying to embarrass her? Prevent her and Wesley from marrying? Disgrace them and, in turn, hurt their families' reputations and businesses?

"Be safe. I will be keeping an eye on you." He pressed a kiss to her temple and raised his voice to Olivia with a nod. "Happy sailing."

Olivia waved.

Amanda squeezed his hand before he pulled away. "You too."

Olivia would have heard it as a polite farewell, but Amanda meant the *be safe* part and tried to convey it to Wesley with her eyes.

He tipped his straw boater hat at Jeffrey and Mr. Gibbons, who acted as his first mate.

Jeffrey dipped his captain's hat in return, but the man looked a bit green.

Heaven help them if the captain got sea sick.

Wesley boarded Bennet's yacht, and the boats set sail, gliding around Narragansett Bay. Amanda gripped the rail and her hat as wind hugged her dress to her body and attempted to pull out the pins and make off with her wide-brimmed sunshade.

Olivia leaned over the rail. "Nothing like the ocean breeze to blow away any remaining dinginess from the city."

Bennett's boat approached on the windward side and Captain Candy's on the leeward. Wesley locked eyes with Amanda. His windblown hair added to his rugged sailor look.

"Let's make a race of it," Bennett yelled above the wind. "Once around Goat Island. Olivia gives the go-ahead."

Jeffrey hesitated but agreed. Mr. Gibbons stood ready to start tacking with Jeffrey at the helm to steer. Olivia moved to the bow and stood tall and proud between the ships with a handkerchief raised. "On your mark. Get set. Go!"

She lowered the scarf, and Mr. Gibbons furiously pulled the line as Jeffrey steered at the helm.

Olivia maneuvered her way back to Amanda, smiling like royalty.

"Blast. Bennett's taking a port-tack approach," Jeffrey yelled to Mr. Gibbons. He turned back to the ladies. "Olivia, watch leeward for the captain's vessel. I can't see the other side of the mainsail. Amanda, stand windward to balance the ship."

Amanda shifted to the other side and grasped the railing as they started to heel. She caught sight of Wesley tacking the sail as their ship assumed the lead. The wind contoured his shirt to his muscular form. For a moment, his gaze met hers and warmth spread to Amanda's cheeks.

"Reef the sail," Jeffrey commanded. "Our flying life-lines are touching water."

"Approaching windward," Olivia yelled and flinched as ocean spray soaked her.

Amanda clung to the rail as the boat tipped to one side.

Jeffrey peeked over his shoulder. "Trim and match their speed."

Too late, one of the other vessels passed them with a salute from Captain Candy.

"Don't pinch the jib. Cut her a little slack."

Their boat fell into last position as the ships cut through the blue waters. Jeffrey and Mr. Gibbons busied themselves trying to regain a better position.

Amanda's stomach flipped as the boat dipped and rose over the wake of the *Candy Man*. Her grip on the rail tightened, and she peered at the bench seat. Could she sit? Or was her help still needed?

"You're letting them get ahead." Olivia frowned at the stern of the *Candy Man*. "There's nothing for me to watch for now. I'm going below deck for a towel to dry off."

"Prepare to jibe around Goat Island," Jeffrey yelled, and Mr. Gibbons moved to the opposite side of the bow.

The sail fell slack for a moment of stillness, and Amanda looked up. The wind caught, and the sails filled quickly, shifting their direction.

The boom hit her in the shoulder and head, wrenching her hand from the rail and sending her flying over the boat's side. She hit the water with a splash. The shocking temperature of the freezing water pushed back the darkness threatening to overtake her. The ocean consumed her in its deep blue-gray and tiny rising bubbles. Her skirts encumbered her legs and weighed her down, but she clawed to rise to the top. She breached the surface and tried to inhale but could only stay above water long enough to release a tiny squeak for help.

She slapped at the water and tilted her chin up as she started to sink. Her lungs sucked in one deep breath before she slipped under the surface and caught sight of a watery image of the *Lucky Turn* continuing without her.

*W*esley peeked over his shoulder before their ship sailed behind Goat Island and he lost sight of Amanda. A tiny lightning bolt of white hit the water, followed by a splash.

"Man overboard!" Wesley yelled and pointed to where he'd spied the splash just before the line of sight was blocked by the isle. "Bring her around." He worked the jib to change direction, and Bennett turned the helm.

Lord, please don't let it be Amanda.

Captain Candy and Longfellow sailed past before realizing he and Bennett were turning and slowed their speed.

"Man overboard!" Wesley yelled again and searched the water for another sign of the figure. How could the ship be going so slow? He leaned over the rail for a better look. Bennett handed him a life ring, and Wesley fumbled for it, refusing to take his gaze off the spot he'd seen the person fall.

Van Hassel spun to look behind him. "Where are Olivia and Amanda?" The wind carried his voice.

A splash and a soggy hat with wilted ostrich feathers emerged from the water.

"There." Wesley pointed at Amanda so the captain could locate her position. As soon as they were within range, he luffed the sail and tossed the life ring.

Amanda reached for it but went under.

Wesley dove overboard.

He opened his eyes under the water. Salt burned, but he caught a flash of white in the murky ocean. He reached her in several strokes and curved an arm around her tiny waist, drawing her against his body. Kicking as hard as he could, he struggled to pull her in her sodden gown to the surface and grabbed the floating life ring. Amanda clung to him and coughed seawater from her lungs.

He gripped her tighter and pressed his cheek to her cold one. "Thank God, you're all right."

Bennett hauled them from the water and went below to grab towels.

Wesley hugged Amanda and rubbed her arms. "I should have been with you. You should have been by my side." *They're getting desperate.* His heart clenched. To the point of murder, or had it been an accident? Amanda was close with the Van Hassels. Surely, they wouldn't harm their friend. Who else was aboard? Gibbons, a few paid crewmen, a staff person. "What happened?"

Amanda peeked over her shoulder and pulled him behind the luffing sail. Was she trying to speak in private?

She touched his cheek and rose onto her toes, but her hand curved around his neck. "Thank you for sailing back for me. I was sinking. I couldn't..." She pressed her cold lips to his despite her chattering teeth.

Wesley's arms tightened around her, forming her perfectly to his body. His mouth moved on hers, sealing his gratefulness for her being alive on her lips. Great Scott, he loved her. If he hadn't looked back one last time, or if he'd lost track of where she'd fallen in...

What if he hadn't gotten to her in time?

He poured his love into his kiss, drawing a soft moan from her throat.

"That's one way to warm up." Bennett chuckled.

Amanda jumped back, and Wesley ached to reel her in again.

Bennett passed him the towels, and Wesley flipped one around Amanda's shoulders. She clasped both corners under her chin.

He sat her on the bench seat before settling his towel on her lap. The wind would dry him fast enough. "What happened?"

"The boat turned, and the boom came around so fast, I couldn't react. I was knocked overboard." Her teeth chattered as she spoke.

"You're certain you weren't pushed?"

She shrugged and shook her head.

Mr. Bennett frowned "The captain didn't call out a warning?"

"Not that I recall."

"Bah. A green mistake." Bennett patted Wesley on the shoulder. "Let's get this ship back into port."

Wesley nodded. The disaster sounded like an accident, but a tumult of questions flooded his mind like a rising tide.

CHAPTER 13

The following afternoon, Amanda escaped Aunt Sally's fussing by retreating to the hot house.

Aunt Sally called after her, "You should be resting. A poor soul could catch her death after such a swim."

Amanda entered the humid room and checked on her orchid. She spritzed it with water, and its magenta flowers bobbed as if dancing with delight.

A potted orange tree sat in a corner with several curled leaves resting in the dirt. Amanda inspected the leaves for mites but thankfully, she found none, for they could spread to other plants. She fixed a special mix with old tea leaves and coffee grounds to restore the tree's pep.

Aunt Sally stood in the hot house doorway and fanned her face from the heat. "Amanda, darling, come. You have more afternoon visitors."

Amanda sighed and pulled off her gardening gloves. Wesley had visited earlier to see how she fared and brought along Detective Millis to hear her retell the tale. The pair of men had reached a truce of sorts since the Gibbons party, and even passed each other knowing looks as if communicating without having to speak. Next time she had a moment alone with Wesley, she would interrogate him about the silent messages.

Amanda stole up the back stairs to her room, where Katie helped her change to receive guests.

Olivia and Jeffrey waited in the blue salon. Olivia paced the room but stopped to greet Amanda with a kiss on each check. "I'm so grateful you aren't feeling any ill effects. Jeffrey and I felt dreadful about the incident. I went below deck for only a moment, and you were gone. Jeffrey assumed I'd called you down and didn't even know you'd fallen overboard until Bennett's boat turned around."

Was that the truth of it?

"Miss Klein." Calvin cleared his throat from the doorway. "You have other visitors." He passed her a card.

She read the beautifully scripted letters twice. Mrs. Caroline Astor and her daughter Carrie.

"Who is it, dear?" Aunt Sally rose and peered over her niece's shoulder.

Olivia did the same. She gripped Amanda's arm and whispered in a strained voice, "You're in. You've done it."

Was that excitement or resentment in her tone? It pained Amanda to be skeptical of her closest friend, but there was no mistaking the tight lines of jealousy in Olivia's smile.

Aunt Sally shoed the butler. "Good heavens. Don't keep them waiting."

"Straighten up, Jeffrey." Olivia scurried to sit next to her husband, lifting her bustle and arranging her skirts.

Mrs. Astor, the notorious queen of New York's high society and her daughter, Carrie, swept into the room, taking the most prominent seats in high-backed chairs like a queen and a princess. The tall ostrich feathers on Mrs. Astor's hat made her appear larger than life. Carrie, while also adorned in the height of fashion, seemed less intimidating as she practically buzzed, eager for all the heroic details of yesterday's rescue.

A fresh pot of tea was served, but Amanda battled to keep her stomach in place like the crabs pulling each other back into the bucket. She recalled Wesley's words, and a peace settled over her. Instead of seeing Mrs. Astor as an intimidating social figure, Amanda looked closer and saw a battle-worn soldier doing her best to stay in the fight.

After almost drowning yesterday, it seemed absurd to be intimidated. Mrs. Astor was probably covering her own insecurities with a haughty exterior. Besides, what could mere man, or in this case woman, do to her if God was with her? Instead of her stomach twisting, now her heart ached for the woman who was loved in the eyes of

God as much as He loved the maid who delivered their tea. Her nervousness dissipated, and she guided the conversation to the matron and daughter's likes and hobbies as she'd often observed Wesley do.

Mrs. Astor chatted amicably for twenty minutes with Amanda. After sipping from her teacup, Mrs. Astor turned her attention to Olivia for the first time. "Do you enjoy hosting parties, Mrs. Van Hassel?"

"I—indeed. I-I do, very much so. We had a ball in New York shortly before coming here with a spring theme." Olivia stumbled over her answer.

"How creative." The twist in Mrs. Astor's lips said otherwise.

The royalty of Newport and New York's elite didn't stay long, but Carrie extended Amanda an invitation to their lawn party.

"Oh, how I adore lawn parties." Olivia turned to her husband, whose mind seemed elsewhere. "Jeffrey too."

"Indeed," he said a mite too quickly.

Carrie started to turn and walk away but glanced Amanda's way. "You should come along, too, then. Since you're a friend of Miss Klein's."

Olivia's face illuminated, and her gloved hand squeezed Jeffrey's forearm.

Aunt Sally saw Mrs. Astor and Carrie to the door.

"To have been singled out by the Astors, what an honor." Olivia released her husband's arm, and Jeffrey shook it out.

Amanda studied her friend of the past few years,

seeing her, too, in a new light—like a naïve infantryman who struggled to please the fellow soldiers when her efforts could be used to please their captain or Lord. Olivia had been a good friend, at least trying to bring Amanda along with her to the top of the bucket. Scripture came to mind, and Amanda spoke it aloud. "'Two people are better off than one, for they can help each other succeed.'"

"That's right." Olivia's eyes glinted. "Remember I got you here." She rose and stared Amanda down. "Don't you dare try and overshadow me."

Her barb struck Amanda to knock her inner crab back down into the bucket, but Amanda was already free. "You've been a good friend, and I'm grateful for all you've done for me. You shine because of who God made you to be, and I can never overshadow that."

Olivia's lips parted, but no words came out. The moment stretched until she snorted and signaled to her husband. "Come along, Jeffrey."

She saw her friend out, then found a quiet corner to pray for forgiveness for being timid, the courage to bloom where she'd been planted, and to love those who so desperately needed it.

The sun had begun to set, and Amanda wandered upstairs to ready for the evening meal.

Katie had a gown of purple taffeta laid out and helped Amanda out of her day dress. She scooped up Amanda's tresses and pinned them into curls at the crown of her head. "Danny went and visited the person

Mr. Jansen recommended, and the man offered him a job as soon as the season's over." Her face radiated with enthusiasm. "Danny thinks we'll have enough funds in a year to have a proper wedding and let an apartment on Mayhew Street away from the riff-raff at the wharf."

"How wonderful, Katie." Amanda smiled back at her in the mirror and reached up, squeezing the maid's hand. "I'm so happy for you both."

"Your Mr. Jansen has a way of seeing potential within people and connecting them."

Amanda's pulse sped at the mention of his name. She liked the way *your Mr. Jansen* sounded. "He does."

He'd drawn Amanda out of her shell and wasn't put off by her shyness and insecurities. Look at the progress he'd helped her make, from the red-dress night, her speaking out in front of the entire room to aid him at the poetry reading, and this afternoon, chatting with Mrs. Astor. He'd helped her build her confidence one small step at a time.

"You won't be venturing out this evening? Won't he be in attendance for the theatre production at The Casino?" Katie tightened the strings on Amanda's corset. "What's being performed?"

"*Vanity Fair*, if I recall. But Wesley is meeting with Detective Millis this evening over this afternoon's events, and I don't have the energy for a social event, not even watching a play."

"It's understandable. My mum's the same way. Poppa used to say that my mum gets wrung out like a rag if she's around too many folks for too long. She needs some quiet time to fill back up before getting back at it again."

Amanda grunted, and Katie pulled the gown over her head and buttoned the buttons. There were other people like herself? It wasn't as if she didn't like people. She enjoyed Wesley's, Katie's, and Olivia's company, but the pressure of having to sustain conversation at parties where people floated in and out—half caring and half listening but at the same time, judging her every sentence and every move and holding expectations— exhausted her.

"It will be nice to dine with your family."

"Indeed." Amanda peered at her maid, an idea blossoming. "I'm staying home and so is my family. It's the perfect night for you and Danny to celebrate his new job offer."

"Truly?" Katie froze as if it was too good to be true. Her chin lowered, and she pulled at the sides of her apron. "I can't. I didn't bring anything to wear."

"We're of a similar size. You can wear one of my gowns."

"Oh miss, I couldn't."

"You have helped me more than you know. Let me do something nice for you."

"God bless you." Katie's eyes misted. "You are a lady of true character."

Amanda strode to the wardrobe and flung open the doors. "Shall we get started, mademoiselle?"

Katie giggled and wiped her eyes with her apron.

"Pick your favorite." She stepped aside, and Katie selected a simple yet lovely pale-green gown with a demi train. Amanda sent a footman to tell Danny he was allowed the night off and to be by the beech tree in one hour. She helped Katie dress but needed instruction to pin her hair into a sleek twist.

Amanda held up a mirror for Katie to see. "You look absolutely stunning."

"I could almost pass for you, as long as I don't stand under the lamplight. My red hair gives me away." Katie gently touched her coiffure.

"Don't give me any ideas." Amanda clasped a small pearl drop necklace around Katie's neck. "Next soirée, I may have you go in my stead." She gripped Katie's shoulders under the puffed sleeves. "Danny is lucky to have you."

"Thank you, miss."

Amanda checked the watch pinned to the front of her gown. Six o'clock. Father wanted an early dinner and would be expecting her. "I mustn't be late for the evening meal."

"I will see you later, Miss Amanda."

"Have a lovely time." Amanda strode to the door. "I'll be waiting up to hear about your night."

Katie waved with a beaming smile on her lips.

Amanda left her bed chamber, scrambling not to be tardy. Dining with her father and Aunt Sally wouldn't likely be restorative, but her heart rejoiced for her friend. If only she could see the surprise on Danny's face when he saw Katie.

⁓

*D*inner had been unexpectedly pleasant, and Amanda lingered longer than she'd anticipated. Instead of her father and aunt pushing her to make social connections, Father harassed Aunt Sally on why marriage plans hadn't been arranged yet.

"Make certain my cousin in California is on the invite list." Father eyed Aunt Sally over his fork.

Aunt Sally's head drew back, creating a double chin. "But Mr. Jansen hasn't officially proposed."

"He's already asked for my blessing, and Amanda hasn't shown interest in other gentlemen."

Aunt Sally's lips pursed. "Your daughter's future isn't a business deal."

"I never said it was." Father set his napkin down next to his plate. "My negotiations were to see what he was willing to sacrifice for Amanda. After saving her life today, I no longer question whether she'll be in good hands. Start planning."

The marriage deal had been a test—not a business transaction? Amanda relaxed in her chair as much as her corset allowed.

He excused himself, rose from the table, and left a bumbling Aunt Sally behind.

"Do you want the wedding in New York or

Newport?" Aunt Sally directed the question at Amanda, but her father answered before the door closed behind him.

"Newport."

Amanda's chest swelled. She'd be married to Wesley before the end of the season.

"Well, then. I guess we should get planning. The reception could be held here. We must reserve Maria De Barril. She'll handle the invitations and schedule Ambrose to do the flower arrangements." Aunt Sally fanned her face. "There's so much to consider."

"And I can't think of anyone more qualified to handle it all." Amanda excused herself before Aunt Sally dragged her into wedding specifics. "Thank you, Aunt Sally, you are a dear."

She forced an unhurried stride from the dining room even though a quiet evening with a book beckoned.

A throat cleared, and a male's shadow stepped from the alcove into the candle-lit hallway.

Amanda jerked to a stop. "Danny." She pressed her hand to her bosom. "You frightened me. Are you and Katie back from dinner?"

"I'm sorry, miss." Danny's face appeared pinched, and he looked both ways. "I'm not supposed to be inside the house, and I don't mean to bother you."

She gripped his arm and walked toward the stairs. "What's wrong?"

"It may be nothin', but Katie never met me where

the footman said, and she isn't answerin' my whistle." He shook out his hands. "It's not like her. Her hearin' is incredible. She usually answers on the first call."

Amanda silenced the alarm blaring in her head. "I saw her before heading to dinner. She was dressed and ready to celebrate your new job offer. Congratulations."

A shy smile played on Danny's lips as if he was unused to compliments.

"Perhaps she dosed off in my dressing room. Let me check my room, and I'll send her down."

"Thank you, miss," Danny said on a whooshed sigh.

Amanda mounted the stairs and strode to her room. *Lord, please let Danny's worries be unfounded.* She opened the door and scanned her chamber. Katie wasn't in the chair. Amanda moved to her dressing room door and swung it wide.

"Katie?"

No answer. Had her maid taken Amanda's day dress to be washed? She exited the room and used the back servant's stairs as a shortcut down two flights to the basement to check with the laundress.

"Is Katie down here?"

"No, miss, I haven't seen her." A hiss and a billow of steam arose as the laundress pressed a hot iron to a pair of Father's slacks.

Where could Katie have gone? Amanda trudged up a flight and peeked out the servant's exit to ask Danny if Katie might have mistaken the beech tree for a different one and was waiting for him in the side yard.

"Miss Klein." A parlor maid was bringing in fresh flowers cut by the gardener to be placed in vases for tomorrow morning. "I thought it was you in that lovely gown, but the gentleman said to find you and tell you to meet him at the back gate."

Amanda put a hand on the back door. "Katie's in the yard with Danny?"

"Not our groomsman, Danny." The parlor maid's brow furrowed. "Oh geez. Did Katie get the boot? The man was kind of hauling her out the back a little rough."

Amanda's stomach plummeted to her silk stockings. Had the person who'd been out to get Amanda mistaken Katie for her? She pushed the door open and yelled for Danny.

Danny rushed over with his driver's hat in his hands.

She gripped Danny's sleeve. "Get Wesley and Detective Millis. Katie's in trouble. I'm going to try to find her." She must find out which way they went while there was still daylight left. "Meet me at the back gate on the cliff walk. Hurry!"

He sprinted for the stables.

Amanda's hands shook. How much time did she have to save Katie? She turned to the maid. "Find my father and have the staff set up a search party."

The maid darted off.

Amanda ran outside, stopping only to grab her bow and quiver from the gardener's shed. Slipping the strap over her head and shoulder, she darted toward the back gate, cutting across the sun-cast tree shadows striping the lawn.

Her breath exhaled in puffs from her quick pace. Beyond the gate, the narrow public walking path skirted rocky outcroppings and bluffs that dipped down into the ocean. Where would Katie's abductor take her? Toward Rosecliff and Ruggles Avenue to a parked carriage, or toward Bailey's beach, where a rowboat might be waiting? She reached the cliff walk entrance, opened the latch, and swung the metal gate wide. The squeaking hinges rusted by the salt spray and ocean air screamed her presence.

Amanda peered down the worn path but didn't see anyone. "Katie?"

A whimpered cry sounded, and Amanda leaned over a low stone wall that guarded passersby from falling down the precipice, ricocheting off protruding rocks before splashing into the ocean. The sea answered with a plume of spray launched into the air and rained sea water on the boulders.

Her maid stood on a rocky ledge near sea level, bound, gagged, and drenched by ocean spray.

"Katie!" Amanda scanned for a means to get to her and any sign of the man who'd abducted her.

A shove sent Amanda tumbling, her scream cut off by a quick jerk of her upper body. She hung suspended by her quiver strap, caught on a thick branch of drift-wood wedged between two rocks a half-body's length below the cliff walk path. Her skirts fluttered and wrapped around her flailing legs as she scrambled for a solid surface. Between the folds of Amanda's hem, about a story's height beneath her slippers, she got glimpses of Katie's tear-streaked face as the maid peered up from the ledge next to swirling inky-black water.

"Blast." The word was spit like a curse from above.

Jeffrey? Amanda glanced up into his spiteful glare. "What is the meaning of—?"

The driftwood cracked and she silenced.

"I'd believed you one clever woman—using your maid as a decoy—and that you'd foiled my plan once again." His head disappeared, and a rope dropped on her left but out of her reach. Hand over hand, he lowered himself down until his Italian leather shoes were level with the driftwood. "But then I remembered you befriend your servants and"—he kicked at the sea-worn branch—"believe them our equals."

The lifesaving piece of wood held, but the jostling swung Amanda side to side. Her foot found a narrow crevice and alleviated some of the strain on the quiver strap.

"If you came for your maid, then my plans weren't thwarted." He kicked harder. "You. Didn't. Disappoint." He punctuated each word with a kick. "It'll look like a rockslide where the two of you drown after a terrible fall." He lost his footing but clung to the rope, bouncing off the rough rocks. "Blast. The only problem is"—he shifted lower and found another foothold—"you won't die. I should have shoved you farther."

God, help. What should I do?

"I don't understand." Wesley's advice to get people talking about themselves flashed in her memory. Would it work? Or at least bide time for help to arrive? "You've always been so kind to me, and your wife is my closest friend."

"You're Olivia's pet project." He reached toward her quiver. "A woman raised by commoners"—his fingers flicked the strap, and it vibrated like a violin string— "and content to live in obscurity"—his voice strained as he stretched—"could never understand the pressure and expectations of high society."

Amanda bristled at Jeffrey referring to Lily, who'd taken Amanda into her home and loved her as though she were her own daughter, as if she were unworthy. "What pressure? You and Olivia are part of the fashionable set, almost as revered as the Astors themselves. Everyone wants to be like you and have what you have. Why would you risk being jailed for murder?"

Another large wave crashed, and Katie whimpered. She clung to the rocks with her bound hands, but the rocky outcrop was slick with green seaweed.

Amanda blinked moisture from her eyes and ignored the strap cutting into her skin. The same length of leather that was her lifeline threatened to pull her arm out of its socket.

"Life is all about risks." Jeffrey's low growl rumbled

with the whitecaps cresting the waves. "My great-grand-father risked coming to America and starting a textile business. I gambled to maintain his fortune in the stock market, but more's at stake now. I need Jansen and Sons stock to plummet because I bet against them. Your breaking off the engagement and therefore the business agreement is crucial for my big payoff." He leaned over the edge farther, and his fingernails scraped the strap of her quiver. His face contorted into a fiendish scowl. "If the union between Klein & Co. and Jansen and Sons stays intact, then I'm ruined. I'll lose everything."

Where was Wesley? *God, please help us.*

Jeffrey climbed the rope so that his feet could once again reach the driftwood.

Amanda moved her bow to grip it between her knees and quickly pulled an arrow from her quiver, careful not to raise the arm that was looped in the strap. Jeffrey turned back to face her, and she quickly hid it in the folds of her cape.

"Olivia, too, wants me dead?"

"My wife knows nothing." Jeffrey kicked the drift-wood. "And I plan to keep it that way."

Amanda gripped the strap tighter as her foot slipped out of the crevice, but the wedged wood held.

"Except for the red dress invitation." He chuckled. "Olivia did that. I believe she wanted to set you down a notch, but it helped my cause, enraging your father, who blamed Jansen. But then Jansen went and wooed Klein back with his conniving tongue."

A wave splashed, followed by a scream as the ocean dragged Katie's body along with its retreat.

"Katie!" Amanda held her breath. *God, please help!*

Katie twisted and was able to hook her tied hands around another rock. Her legs dangled in the water, and her skirts billowed with each swell.

Amanda turned to Jeffrey. "Please save her. She has nothing to do with this. You have me. She's just a maid."

"And ruin my Italian leather shoes? I paid more for them than she's worth."

A chill ran over Amanda's skin. Jeffrey Van Hassel not only thought himself above them, but he also didn't value the sanctity of life.

He grabbed the strap, and placing his elbow against the rock for leverage, attempted to lift her weight and slide the strap down the piece of driftwood. He succeeded by a few inches.

"Amanda!" Wesley's voice rang like a reinforcement cavalryman's call.

"Wesley!" *Thank you, Lord.*

"Blast," Jeffrey whispered. He climbed up, pinning his back against the rocks she'd fallen from.

Did he think to hide? He'd easily be spotted. Amanda's breath caught as Jeffrey peered up, hands ready to yank Wesley over the edge.

"Wesley, stay where you are." She fumbled for her bow, trying to raise it into position and not slip through the strap's hold. The arrow nearly slipped from her fingers, but she notched it and tilted the arrow up.

"Amanda!" Wesley peered over the wall. Spotting her, his eyes widened.

She focused her mark on Jeffrey's shoulder, exhaled, and shot her arrow. The released force unhooked her arm, and she slid loose.

Jeffrey shrieked.

Amanda's fingers clasped the strap. She dangled, twisting and ricocheting off hard rocks. Her bow splashed into the water beside Katie.

Small pebbles bounced off the top of Amanda's head. She glanced up to see Jeffrey with her arrow protruding from just below his collarbone. He stumbled about, trying to remove the arrow, and Amanda flinched as more pebbles rained down.

Wesley swiped an arm but missed him. Detective Millis caught Jeffrey's collar and yanked him over the rock barrier. "You're under arrest for attempted murder." He pinned Jeffrey's arms behind his back, and he whimpered.

Amanda's slipper soles scraped the rock cliff, and her arms shook, trying to maintain her grasp on the quiver strap.

The ocean breeze carried Katie's muffled scream.

"I'm coming for you, Katie-girl." Danny launched over the wall with a cord used to train horses tied around his waist.

"Mandi Mae." Wesley descended using Jeffrey's rope. His strong arm curled around her waist and gruffly hauled her against his chest.

She clung to him, inhaling his masculine scent.

"I've got you." He pressed a rough kiss to her cheek and shifted her around to his back so he could climb up the precipice.

Detective Millis aided her and Wesley over the wall. Jeffrey stood behind him handcuffed to the metal gate leading to Breakwater Court. Blood seeped through his expensive white custom-tailored shirt.

As soon as Wesley stood on solid ground, Amanda threw herself into his embrace.

"Nice shot, Mandi Mae," Wesley said into her hair, "but don't ever risk your life like that again."

"He was going to yank you over the edge." She pressed her face into his neck and squeezed him tight. "I love you too much to lose you."

"I love you too. More than my own life." He reluctantly released her and helped the detective pull Danny and Katie up.

Wesley handed Katie over the wall to Amanda, and she untied Katie's gag and picked at the knots binding her hands until they fell away.

"Miss, you came for me."

"Of course. You're my friend." Amanda wrapped Katie in a hug.

Wesley helped Danny over the wall and clapped him on the back. Danny shook his hand before turning and embracing Katie.

Detective Millis hopped over the wall and wiped his forehead with his sleeve.

"Your hunch was right." Wesley nodded to the detective and pulled Amanda against his side, pressing another kiss to her temple. She leaned into his protection.

A gathered search party of staff approached the open back gate, and Jeffrey hung his head, hiding his face.

The detective moved to the gate and reclaimed his captive. "He had the most to lose once he bet his fortune, shorting Jansen and Sons' stock. Once the companies merge through the marriage agreement, he'll lose everything."

Amanda whispered to Wesley, "Olivia said he'd been listening at the door when you asked Father for his blessing."

Wesley stiffened. "He'd also been seen with Cynthia Blunt the night of the party."

Detective Millis signaled a footman to grip Jeffrey's other arm, and they started toward the carriage. "You not only failed at avoiding financial ruin, but you also now owe a greater debt to society. I'm thinking the judge will give you sixty to life in prison, and your tux will be traded in for a black-and-white-striped jumpsuit."

"Thank you, miss, for helping me locate Katie." Danny could hardly take his eyes off his girl. "I don't know many employers who'd stick their necks out like that to save the help."

"I prayed for this job, and God blessed me with Miss

Klein." Katie glanced at Jeffrey's retreating form. "He planned to drown you and make it look like suicide, but then he mistook me for you and was livid. He revised his plan to drown us both and kept sayin' you're the only mistress who'd help a servant." A visible shiver ran through her body. "He thought no more of my life than he would an old newspaper to be thrown in the trash."

Danny folded Katie in his arms. "You are more valuable to me than all the money in all of Newport." He stepped back. "Come on, let's get you dried off. I can't have you catching your death after saving your life."

Amanda moved to follow them, but Wesley tugged her back.

His hands slid up her arms and cradled her head. His eyes glistened in the moonlight. He glanced heavenward and whispered a hoarse, "Thank you, Lord."

She tugged on the lapel of his jacket before toying with the hair at the nape of his neck.

Wesley's mouth claimed hers with a soul-baring hunger that couldn't have been expressed in words. Amanda returned his kiss with a passion of her own and a gratefulness to God for bringing Wesley, Katie, and Danny into her life.

A person's value didn't come from their bank account, bloodlines, or social connections. Their worth was determined by those they loved and who loved them in return and by God, who gave His son so they could have life. And she planned to live it to the full.

Wesley pulled back and rested his forehead against hers. "Marry me, Mandi Mae."

She brushed her lips against his, savoring the velvety-smooth feel, and smiled against his mouth. "That's a capital idea."

Did you enjoy this book? We hope so!
**Would you take a quick minute to leave a review
where you purchased the book?**
It doesn't have to be long. Just a sentence or two telling
what you liked about the story!

Receive a FREE ebook and get updates when new Wild
Heart books release: https://wildheartbooks.org/
newsletter

GLOSSARY

Glossary of real Gilded Age Newport residents and guests with cameos in *A Summer on Bellevue Avenue*:

Caroline Schermerhorn Astor – Prominent American heiress and New York knickerbocker socialite married to William Backhouse Astor Jr. The Astor family summered at their "cottage," the Beechwood, in Newport, RI. Their ballroom on Fifth Avenue in New York City was considered society's inner sanctum, and invitations were scarce and coveted.

Carrie Astor – Caroline Astor's youngest daughter, Carrie, married Marshall Orme Wilson. The young socialite pleaded with her mother to call upon Alva Vanderbilt so she could attend Alva's costume party. Mrs. Astor's visit meant Alva Vanderbilt had "arrived" and was accepted into the knickerbocker society.

James Gordon Bennett Jr. – Publisher of the *New York Herald* and founder of the Newport Casino social and sporting club on Bellevue Avenue, James Bennet was an avid sportsman. He won the first trans-oceanic yacht race and established the first polo match in the United States.

Maria De Barril – Newport's social executive assistant who managed the social lives of Newport's rich, Maria De Barril, had been born into a privileged society as a wealthy South American heiress but was left destitute after the 1893 stock market crash. She put her social skills and connections to good use by managing the social lives of Newport's elite. Her recognizable penmanship on invitations meant the party was an upper-echelon event.

Captain Henry "Sugar" Candy – Friend of James Gordon Bennett Jr., captain, and polo player, Sugar was a summer member of the men's Reading Room club. However, on a prank instigated by Bennett, Sugar rode his horse up the club's front steps and wound up being chastised for it.

Marion "Mammie" Graves Anthon Fish – Mammie married her

childhood sweetheart, Stuyvesant Fish, president of the IL Central Railroad. She and her husband summered at Crossways in Newport, RI. Mammie is most famous for her sharp tongue and outlandish parties, like dining on horseback or a barn dance where the guests dressed as servants and the servants dressed as the guests.

Elizabeth Drexel Lehr – Banking heiress and Manhattan socialite married Henry Lehr after the death of her first husband, John Vinton Dahlgren. Her second marriage was an unhappy one. In her semi-autobiographical novel, *"King Lehr" and the Gilded Age,* she claims on her wedding night, her husband declared, "I do not love you. I can never love you." The couple kept up their tragic sham of a marriage for public appearances.

Charles Longfellow – Son of American Poet Henry Wadsworth Longfellow, Charley was a sojourner of foreign cultures and a yachting enthusiast where he befriended James Gordon Bennett Jr.

Theresa "Tessie" Fair Oelrichs – A San Francisco, CA silver mine heiress who made her social debut in Newport, RI, and married a steamship tycoon, Hermann Oelrich. After the wedding, Tessie purchased and resided at Rosecliff in Newport, RI, while her husband preferred San Francisco and rarely spent time with his wife. During an era when the tiny wasp waist was in fashion, Tessie struggled with a fluctuating weight problem, often squeezing her waistline with sinched corsets. Her tendency toward cleanliness and perfectionism proved beneficial as head of the Newport Social Strategy Board alongside Mamie Fish and Alva Vanderbilt.

Alva Smith Vanderbilt – Rescued her family from a financial crisis by marrying William K. Vanderbilt, the wealthy son of steamship and railroad mogul Commodore Vanderbilt. Alva wrestled her way up the social ladder by building Marble House in Newport, RI, and then tricking Caroline Astor into giving the new money Vanderbilts her approval. Alva hosted a masquerade ball in honor of Viscountess Mandeville, and it was to be an A-list party. Carrie Astor became distraught when she didn't receive an invitation and persuaded her mother, Caroline Astor, to accept the Vanderbilts into their inner sanctum of social elites.

Consuela Vanderbilt – Daughter to Alva and William Vanderbilt, Consuela was one of the wealthy American "dollar princess" who was married off to Edwin William Spencer-Churchill, the Duke of Marlborough, as a business transaction—her dowry for an English title. Consuela was in love with a knickerbocker bachelor, Winthrop Rutherford, and refused to marry the duke. At least, until her mother, Alva Vanderbilt, feigned an illness from which she suspiciously recovered as Consuela wed the duke.

Information gathered thanks to the Newport Mansions Preservation Society and Davis, Deborah, *Gilded: How Newport Became America's Richest Resort*, Hoboken, NJ, John Wiley & Sons, 2009.

Don't miss the next book in the Romance at the Gilded Age Resorts Series!

A Spring at the Greenbrier
By Sandra Merville Hart

Chapter 1

MARCH 12, 1914
WHITE SULPHUR SPRINGS, WEST VIRGINIA

"It smells like rotten eggs." Ten-year-old Katie Stevens pinched her nose.

"I sympathize." Marilla Stevens lifted her sister from her wheelchair into the tub filled with warm sulphur spring water. Because Marilla's income didn't stretch to purchase a bathing costume, Katie wore a petticoat that billowed to the water line. "The odor is something one must grow accustomed to." She'd switched jobs at The Greenbrier last month to the Bath Wing, where guests of the resort bathed in the spring waters. The aroma no longer bothered her. Katie had only been taking the baths for four days.

"Quite right. It's not worth complaining about, not when Dr. Bruening hopes bathing daily in the waters may benefit you." Mama carried a chair across the spacious room to the tub. Tendrils of black hair streaked with gray curled against her forehead. Her green wool dress accentuated her trim figure. "Mind you, keep your hair dry. We can't have you riding home with wet hair in the frosty breeze."

They shielded her sister from every illness within their power. Marilla bent to retrieve a change of clothing and towels from Mama's old carpetbag beside the wheelchair. She and Mama were determined not to use any of the resort's supplies beyond the facilities.

Katie lifted her blond pigtails over the lip of the tub. "It'd be nice to walk again. I hardly remember what it feels like to get around without the chair."

Marilla sucked in her breath. Her sister had rarely indulged in melancholy in the three years polio had stolen her ability to walk. Though bathing in sulphur springs seemed a far-fetched hope, anything was worth a try. Her initial job after last September's reopening of The Greenbrier had been serving glasses of cold spring water to guests, many of whom drank it before every meal. That task had been far less exhausting than her current position. Still, it was worth the sacrifice if the baths, known to ease or even heal some conditions, strengthened her sister's legs.

"You'll walk again someday." Mama extracted her latest knitting project—a shawl for Katie—from her bag beside the wheelchair. Frances Stevens had never wavered from that belief, even when Papa died two years ago from a heart attack.

"I'll be able to climb the steps to the schoolhouse. I'll read books with other students. Do sums on the blackboard." Katie closed her blue eyes as if imagining

SNEAK PEEK: A SPRING AT THE GREENBRIER

it all. "I'll make new friends at school. They'll play tag with me at recess."

Marilla turned away. School wasn't possible while Katie required a wheelchair. Not only for the steps but also for maneuvering the wheels over the rutted, sloped path to the privy. The teacher couldn't carry her up the steps nor accompany her to the privy every time.

"Marilla, do you think the girls from my class will attend my birthday party in June?"

"We'll see." Marilla wished Mama would refrain from giving Katie hope of walking again. Marilla had learned the hard way to forget her dreams. At twenty, a woman might expect to marry, raise a family of her own. That wasn't possible for her. Caring for Katie required sacrifices from both her and her mother. No man wanted the burden of providing for Marilla's family.

"Most assuredly. Your friends will come." Mama raised her eyebrows at Marilla.

"Then the smell is worth it." Katie grinned.

Marilla dipped her fingers into the water. Maintaining a constant temperature was crucial. "Let's warm it up." As she leaned forward to allow hot steam to enter the tub from -----, she stifled a groan. The warmth would surely also benefit a back that ached from lifting or assisting folks into the tub all day.

No matter. After all, this treatment wasn't for her. The family was fortunate that Marilla's boss, Lena Cochran, allowed Katie to bathe after the guests finished. Lena's stipulation was that Marilla cleaned up the room afterward and didn't fuss about it to her coworkers and especially the guests. If folks complained, the precious privilege was likely to be revoked.

A risk Marilla could not afford, for her salary barely stretched to buy necessities and pay the doctor. By no means could she pay for daily bathing sessions at the expensive resort.

Weston Bakersfield stepped off the horse-drawn omnibus that had shuttled him from the railroad depot to The Greenbrier's main entrance. His mother, who had arrived with his three sisters on Monday, had written that they were in the same suite of rooms as previously.

"May I see to your trunk, sir?" One of the men bedecked in black-suited finery from a bygone era stepped forward.

"Yes, thank you." He provided the room number as he searched the portico for his family. No sign of them. Good, he needed a brisk walk after that long train journey that began before breakfast. There was time to walk to the stables, as was his custom on travel days, and still return in time to dress for supper.

Buttoning his frock coat against the chilly breeze, he set off at a rapid pace. Accustomed as he was to active days at his family's carriage factories, he was glad for a slower pace at The Greenbrier. The Old White, as it was affectionately called, had become an expensive home away from home due to Ina's, his nine-year-old sister's, need to bathe in the waters. Pain from her bouts with juvenile rheumatoid arthritis was eased after a couple of weeks. Mama had decided to extend their stay to four weeks this time to see if the healing effects lasted longer. She'd hired a tutor for his younger sisters and brought along Ina's companion because their stay lasted through the Easter holidays.

Wes couldn't afford to neglect his management of four of their carriage factories and planned to join his family for the weekends. Papa had enlisted a partner experienced in manufacturing cars to help him convert their Richmond factory.

He shoved his hands in his pockets. Papa apparently never considered including Wes in the company's new direction—one that he'd convinced his father to consider because the future of transportation steered toward motor cars. True, a mere handful of cars dotted the landscape outside the resort's cottages. Only thirteen people out of a thousand owned a car. The rest either couldn't afford one or preferred horse-drawn vehicles.

Why didn't his father include him on the changes from the beginning? They'd both learn together what must be done.

A woman and a girl about Ina's age waited outside

the Bath Wing near a bed of blue violets, perhaps to enjoy the flowers' delicate fragrance. Unlike Ina, this girl was in a wheelchair. The part of her blue floral print dress not covered by a white shawl wasn't the expensive fabric worn by his sisters or guests of the resort. Its appearance was more what children wore in town.

Was she here to partake of the waters in hopes of walking again? His heart went out to both mother and daughter as he passed them. They didn't spare him a glance. Their attention was fixed on a lone figure ahead.

Something in the slump of the young woman's shoulders ignited his compassion, just as the little girl in the wheelchair had done. Her black dress was the familiar garb of resort workers. If she was helping the family, perhaps he could be of some assistance. He lengthened his stride.

Despite apparent exhaustion, the woman walked with purpose. She reached the stables ahead of him.

"Mr. Feldman, I'm here for my family's wagon." Marilla stepped just inside the long, dank stable.

"Sorry, Miss Marilla." A black man in his late twenties ducked his head out of a stall. "Gotta saddle six horses for guests. Can you wait?"

"No worries. I'll hitch Betsy to my wagon." She'd done it often enough since Papa died. The stable hand knew about her sister and had hitched their horse in record time all week, a privilege she must not take for granted.

"Ole Betsy ate some oats. That mare enjoyed her early supper."

"Thank you, kindly." A treat indeed, for it stretched their feed for another day.

Grinning at her, he ducked back into the stall.

Other stable hands milled about the building while Marilla led her mare outside to their old wagon that seemed out of place in front of the buggies and carriages housed in their temporary home.

"Good afternoon."

Marilla spun around at the deep, unfamiliar voice. The tall man's expensive frock coat, derby hat, and shiny leather shoes hinted that the handsome stranger was a guest of the resort. Had he followed her? She maneuvered Betsy between them.

"Might I assist you in harnessing your horse?" He halted several paces from her. "My name's Weston Bakersfield. I just got off the train and wanted a bit of exercise."

Of the Bakersfield Carriage Company? They had factories in Virginia and West Virginia. "Marilla Stevens. A pleasure." She glanced at her black dress and ruffled apron peeking from underneath her drab brown shawl. No need to mention she worked here. If he was a resort guest, her uniform proclaimed that wordlessly. Why did he want to risk getting his shoes dirty by hitching her horse? However, it was a task she didn't enjoy.

"May I?" He held out his hand.

"If you like." She gave him Betsy's halter.

"My family is staying at the resort. My youngest sister benefits from bathing in the waters." Mr. Bakersfield positioned the mare in front of the old buckboard.

That caught her attention. "I work in the Bath Wing. How old is your sister?"

"Ina is nine."

"She came with her mother today." She'd climbed into the tub holding Marilla's hand, one of her easiest patrons all day. "She's on my schedule tomorrow."

"Glad to hear Ina is in capable hands." He smoothed the straps over the horse.

Such a compliment was a rarity for her. Warmth spread in her cheeks.

"We get orders for many farmers' wagons at our carriage company." He arranged the reins over the seat. "Lots of demand for them. Won't go out of production for years."

So she'd guessed correctly. If his family could stay at the resort, they must be wealthy. "I must get back to pick up my mother and sister. They're waiting for me."

"I believe I saw them near the Bath Wing entrance." He extended his hand to help her onto the seat.

"Thank you." She accepted it, feeling his strength. This man didn't just sit behind a desk—he toiled. She released his hand quickly and couldn't help but remember it'd been two years since a man helped her climb onto a vehicle.

"My pleasure." He touched the brim of his gray hat. "Does your sister partake of the waters?"

Lucky guess? She mustn't confirm it. "Thank you for your assistance, Mr. Bakersfield. Good day." She drove off before he responded.

He'd treated her, a resort worker guests only noticed when needing her services, like a lady. He was a gentleman. How she longed for someone kind and considerate to court her. Take her to church and picnics along the Greenbrier River. Someone who would help her shoulder her family responsibilities.

Marilla tilted her chin. Indulging in that dream could only bring disappointment. Richard Renquist had taught her that lesson.

ABOUT THE AUTHOR

Lorri Dudley has been a finalist in numerous writing contests and has a master's degree in Psychology. She lives in Ashland, Massachusetts with her husband and three teenage sons, where writing romance allows her an escape from her testosterone filled household.

Website: http://lorridudley.com

   BookBub: https://www.bookbub.com/authors/lorri-dudley

   Facebook: https://facebook.com/lorri.dudley.14

   Pinterest: https://pinterest.com/lorridudley14/

   Instagram: https://instagram.com/lorridudley/?hl=en

ACKNOWLEDGMENTS

Thank you to Misty Beller and Wild Heart Books for putting together this series. I'm blessed to be part of such a great publishing house with supportive authors. A special thanks to Robyn Hook and Denise Weimer for your feedback and editing skills. I appreciate you having my blind spots.

I owe a debt of gratitude to Kristen Carlson for her sailing wisdom and revisions to my sailboat racing scenes. Also her husband, Nik, and Courtney Beard for their passion for sailing and input. A special thanks also to the Preservation Society of Newport County, my beta readers, and a big shout out to my launch team.

To my family and friends, I love you. Thank you for all your support in my writing journey.

And especially to God, to You goes all the glory!

The Agents of Espionage Series

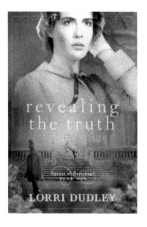

Book 1: Revealing the Truth

Book 2: Reclaiming the Spy

The Leeward Island Series

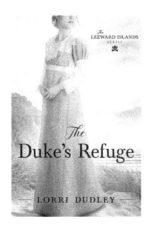

Book 1: The Duke's Refuge

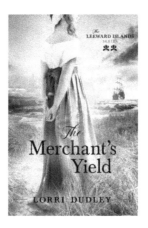

Book 2: The Merchant's Yield

Book 3: The Sugar Baron's Ring

Book 4: The Captain's Quest

Book 5: The Marquis's Pursuit

Book 6: The Heir's Predicament

Want more?

If you love historical romance, check out the other Wild Heart books!

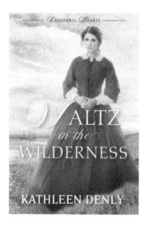

Waltz in the Wilderness by Kathleen Denly

She's desperate to find her missing father. His conscience demands he risk all to help.

Eliza Brooks is haunted by her role in her mother's death, so she'll do anything to find her missing pa—even if it means sneaking aboard a southbound ship. When those meant to protect her abandon and betray her instead, a family friend's unexpected assistance is a blessing she can't refuse.

Daniel Clarke came to California to make his fortune, and a stable job as a San Francisco carpenter has earned him more than most have scraped from the local goldfields. But it's been four years since he left Massachusetts and his fiancé is impatient for his return. Bound for home at last, Daniel Clarke finds his heart and plans challenged by a tenacious young woman with haunted eyes. Though every word he utters seems to offend her, he is determined to see her safely returned to her father. Even if that means risking his fragile engagement.

When disaster befalls them in the remote wilderness of the Southern California mountains, true feelings are revealed, and both must face heart-rending decisions. But how to decide when every choice before them leads to someone getting hurt?

~

A Matter of Trust by Winnie Griggs

When Lucy Ames rescues a stranger from being beaten and robbed, she can't just leave the man to die, but with her reputation in town already in tatters, how can she take this wounded man into her home? All she can do is what's right...and hope for the best. Unlike Lucy, her young charge, Toby, is delighted to have a man in the house. As much as Lucy wants the man gone, she can't begrudge him the father figure he never knew.

On a self-assigned mission to locate his nephew, Reed Wilder can't believe his luck when he realizes his beautiful rescuer is the strumpet who beguiled his arrow-straight brother. But she's not at all what he expected. She's independent and feisty and...captivating. Before either of them realize it, Lucy and Reed fall in love. But how can their relationship survive the secrets that plague them both?

∾

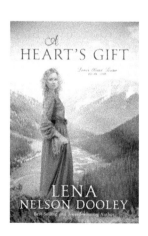

A Heart's Gift by Lena Nelson Dooley

Is a marriage of convenience the answer?

Franklin Vine has worked hard to build the ranch he inherited into one of the most successful in the majestic Colorado mountains. If only he had an heir to one day inherit the legacy he's building. But he was burned once in the worst way, and he doesn't plan to open his heart to another woman. Even if that means he'll eventually have to divide up his spread among the most loyal of his hired hands.

When Lorinda Sullivan is finally out from under the control of men who made all the decisions in her life, she promises herself she'll never allow a man to make choices for her again. But without a home in the midst of a hard Rocky Mountain winter, she has to do something to provide for her infant son.

A marriage of convenience seems like the perfect arrangement, yet the stakes quickly become much higher than either of them ever planned. When hearts become entangled, the increasing danger may change their lives forever.